. . . *Grandpa's apron,* filled with surprises,
the biggest of all reserved for
Grandpa himself!

. . . *The button basket,* chock-full of wonder
even when empty . . . beaded legacy of
a starving Indian who traded his past
for a loaf of bread

. . . *Little gray shoes,* too expensive at any
price—but painfully tempting

. . . *The new pump;* it inspired a dare that
nearly froze young Grandma's tongue

. . . *Ma's birthday cake,* flavored with
her daughter's love . . . and with
Watkin's Liniment!

Laugh, enjoy, and read on.
. . . You're never too old
for a good story!

In Grandma's Attic

Arleta Richardson

Illustrated by Dora Leder

IN GRANDMA'S ATTIC
Copyright © 1974 David C. Cook Publishing Co.

First printing, June 1974
Seventeenth printing, April 1983
Eighteenth printing, November 1983
Nineteenth printing, March 1984

David C. Cook Publishing Co., Elgin, IL 60120

Printed in the United States of America
Library of Congress Catalog Number: 74-75541

ISBN: 0-912692-32-4

The stories in this book appeared previously in "Story Trails," Light
and Life Press; "Junior Trails," Assemblies of God; "Words of
Cheer," Mennonite Publishing House; and in "Bible Truth," Chris-
tian Reformed Church.

Introduction

"TELL ME ABOUT when you were a little girl."

Have you ever said that to your mother or grandmother? I did, and I was fortunate enough to have a Grandma who could make stories come alive. Now when my children at school or church ask for a story, I say, "Let me tell you some stories I used to hear when I was a little girl your age." Then I tell them about old Nellie and her trips to town, or a cow named Molly Blue, or the Indian who came out of the woods.

I wish you could have known Grandma. You would have loved her. She was born just one hundred years ago on a little farm in Michigan.

One hundred years! What a long, long time ago! Is it hard to imagine anyone that old ever being a little girl? But of course she was, and she remembered it very well.

I never saw the little log house where Grandma was born, but I can imagine how it looked. It had one big room that was warmed by a fireplace and a big cookstove. Her brothers slept in a loft overhead, and Grandma slept in a trundle-bed beside her parents. (That is a little cot that slides under the big bed during the day.) The cabin sat in a small clearing in the woods, and even though there were no neighbors near, the family felt safe and protected in their little home.

By the time Grandma was ready to go to school, the log cabin had been replaced by the big farmhouse that still stood when I was a little girl.

The trips to Grandma's old home were the most fun I could have. I explored from the attic to the root cellar, and from the barn to the meadow brook. Everywhere I looked I found a story!

The attic was dusty and creaky, but what marvelous things it contained! A funny-looking wire thing that turned out to be something to wear. A slate with a hard pencil to write on it. (Grandma had carried that to school.)

And in the old trunk, quilt pieces that Grandma and I put together for my bed. There was a red velvet square that had been part of a bonnet, a flowered piece that was a birthday dress, a heavy square that had been an apron with many pockets—and so many more. Was there a story to go with each of those things? Well, I guess so!

The old house was really a big storybook. The "summer" kitchen held the big wood stove that had warmed the room. The china cabinet held the Button Basket, and I couldn't take the cover off *that* without a story jumping out!

Then the barn was still there, with lots more interesting things to look at. Nellie's harness hanging behind the stall. The buggy that Grandma had lost! An old door leaning up against the wall. A big, rusty hook that sent Grandpa flying out over the barn floor.

But, enough of that. I expect that you would like to hear the stories that Grandma told, wouldn't you? I just happened to be the little girl she told them to *almost* fifty years ago, but you can enjoy them now every bit as much as I did then.

Los Angeles, California　　　　　　　　ARLETA RICHARDSON

THE STORIES
Page

1	Pride Goes Before a Fall	11
2	When God Knew Best	15
3	The Red Bonnet	19
4	Grandpa's Apron	23
5	Ma's Busy Day	27
6	Grandma's Mistake	31
7	The Button Basket	35
8	The Little Gray Shoes	39
9	Nellie and the Buttons	44
10	The Pearl Buttons	48
11	Nellie's Trips to Town	52
12	The New Pump	58
13	You Can't Always Believe	62
14	The Old Door	66
15	Pa and the Dishwater	70
16	The Dishes	74
17	Ma's Birthday Cake	79
18	Grandma's Warm Clothes	85
19	Grandma's Prayer	89
20	Molly Blue	93
21	Grandma and the Gun	97
22	What Grandma Lost	100
23	What Did You Expect?	107

In Grandma's
Attic

1

Pride Goes Before a Fall

"GRANDMA, what is this?"

Grandma looked up from her work.

"Good lands, child, where did you find that?"

"In the attic," I replied. "What is it, Grandma?"

Grandma chuckled and answered, "That's a hoop. The kind ladies wore under their skirts when I was a little girl."

"Did you ever wear one, Grandma?" I asked.

Grandma laughed. "Indeed I did," she said. "In fact, I wore that very one."

Here, I decided, must be a story. I pulled up the footstool and prepared to listen. Grandma looked at the old hoop fondly.

"I only wore it once," she began. "But I kept it to remind me how painful pride can be.

"I was about eight years old when that hoop came into my life. For months I had been begging Ma to let me have a hoop skirt like the big girls wore. Of course, that was out of the question. What would a little girl, not even out of calicos, be doing with a hoop skirt? Nevertheless, I could envision myself walking haughtily to school with a hoop skirt and having all the girls watching enviously as I took my seat in the front of the room.

"This dream was shared by my best friend and seatmate, Sarah Jane. Together we spent many hours picturing ourselves as fashionable young ladies in ruffles and petticoats. But try as we would, we could not come up with a single plan for getting a hoop skirt of our very own.

"Finally, one day in early spring, Sarah Jane met me at the school grounds with exciting news. An older cousin had come to their house to visit, and she had two old hoops that she didn't want any longer. Sarah Jane and I could have them to play with, she said. Play with indeed! Little did that cousin know that we didn't want to *play* with them! Here was the answer to our dreams. All day, under cover of our books, Sarah Jane and I planned how we would wear those hoops to church on Sunday.

"There was a small problem. How would I get that hoop into the house without Ma knowing about it? And how could either of us get out of the house with them on when no one could see us? It was finally decided that I would stop by Sarah Jane's house on Sunday morning. We would have some excuse for walking to church, and after her family had left, we would put on our hoops and prepare to make a grand entrance at the church.

" 'Be sure to wear your fullest skirt,' Sarah Jane reminded me. 'And be here early. They're all sure to look at us this Sunday!' If we had only known how true that would be! But of course, we were happily unaware of the disaster that lay ahead.

"Sunday morning came at last, and I astonished my family by the speed with which I finished my chores and was ready to leave for church.

" 'I'm going with Sarah Jane this morning,' I announced, and set out quickly before there was any protest.

"All went according to plan. Sarah Jane's family went on in the buggy cautioning us to hurry, and not be late for service. We did have a bit of trouble fastening the hoops around our waists and getting our skirts pulled down to cover them. But when finally we were ready, we agreed that there could not be two finer looking young ladies in the county than we were.

"Quickly we set out for church, our fine hoop skirts swinging as we walked. Everyone had gone in when we arrived, so we were assured of the grand entry we desired. Proudly, with small noses tipped up, we sauntered to the front of the church and took our seats.

"Alas! No one had ever told us the hazards of sitting down in a hoop skirt without careful practice! The gasps we heard were not of admiration as we had anticipated —far from it! For when we sat down, those dreadful hoops flew straight up in the air! Our skirts covered our faces, and the startled minister was treated to the sight of two pairs of white pantalettes and flying petticoats.

"Sarah Jane and I were too startled to know how to disentangle ourselves, but our mothers were not. Ma quickly snatched me from the seat and marched me out the door.

"The trip home was a silent one. My dread grew with each step. What terrible punishment would I receive at the hands of an embarrassed and upset parent? Although I didn't dare look at her, I knew she was upset, because she was shaking. It was to be many years before I learned that Ma was shaking from laughter, and not from anger!

"Nevertheless, punishment was in order. My Sunday afternoon was spent with the big Bible and Pa's concordance. My task was to copy each verse I could find that had to do with being proud. It was a sorry little girl who learned a lesson about pride going before a fall that day."

The story was ended.

"And you were never proud again, Grandma?" I asked.

Grandma thought soberly for a moment. "Yes," she replied. "I was proud again. Many times. It was not until I was a young lady and the Lord saved me, that I had the pride taken from my heart. But many times when I am tempted to be proud, I remember that horrid hoop skirt, and decide that a proud heart is an abomination to the Lord!"

2

When God Knew Best

MY DAY WAS RUINED. I had been promised a trip, and one of those freak sudden spring storms had come in the night. The ground was covered with snow, and more was falling. Of course we couldn't drive to the city in a storm. I could understand that, couldn't I?

I couldn't. As I poked moodily at my cereal, Grandma bustled cheerfully around the kitchen. How could she be so happy when my whole day lay in bits around my feet?

"What can I do all day? No one can even come to play. How come it had to storm today? It just isn't fair!" I complained.

"Well, child," Grandma replied. "The Lord has a reason for changing your plans. He always knows what is best for us."

This I doubted, but since Grandma was so much better acquainted with the Lord than I was, I didn't like to dispute her. I could see no possible reason for a disappointment like this, and if the Lord did have one, He wasn't telling it to me.

Finally finished with breakfast, I stared grumpily out the window. Grandma's voice broke into my unhappy thoughts.

"I'm going to tie a quilt today. Maybe you'd like to help."

That would be better than nothing, I guessed. The quilt was laid out on the big table and the yarn for tying it was threaded in big needles. In spite of myself, I found the bright colored quilt pieces fascinating.

"Look, Grandma," I exclaimed. "Isn't this a piece of your dress? I remember it when I was just little. I tried to pick the flowers off in church!"

Grandma laughed. "Yes, that was my dress all right. And here's a piece of your uncle's first suit with long pants. Oh how proud he was of that suit. And here's your mother's first school pinafore."

"This one is pretty, Grandma. What did it come from?"

Grandma looked at the square of lavender cotton with small white flowers on it.

"Why, that is a piece of my Birthday Dress," she replied. "I'd almost forgotten about that."

"Which birthday, Grandma? You've had a lot of them."

"Yes," replied Grandma. "I've had a lot of them, but never one like that one. I was twelve years old that year, two years older than you are."

"Tell me about it, Grandma," I begged. "What made that birthday so special?"

Grandma thought quietly for a moment, then she began.

"My birthday came in June. We didn't have much money in the summer. Pa depended on good crops in the fall to supply the money for things we needed and couldn't grow on the farm. But this year, Ma had a surprise for me. She had bought this piece of goods the fall before, and saved it for a dress for summer.

"Oh, it was a pretty dress. There were tiny tucks in the waist, and Ma had put handmade lace around the neck and sleeves. I had never had such a wonderful dress. And it was to be worn on my birthday for a very special occasion. The all-day picnic was to be held in Carter's Grove about ten miles from our home. I would see all my best friends and have a whole glorious day with no chores to worry about.

"The dress was hung where I could see it as I helped Ma get the food ready for the picnic. I was so excited that I wasn't really much help, but Ma understood how I felt. I dreamed of nothing but that picnic and the new dress.

"The night before the big day, I began to feel funny. My throat scratched and my head hurt. I thought it best not to say anything to Ma, however. Nothing was going to spoil that picnic. But when morning came, the dreadful truth was known. I was sick. I struggled bravely to the table, but Ma took one look and announced, 'Mabel has the measles, Pa. You'll have to take the boys and go on to the picnic. I'll stay home with her.'

"Oh, what a terrible disappointment! Not to be able to wear that beautiful dress, or see my friends, or celebrate my birthday!

"Ma did her best to comfort me, but I would not be comforted. 'The Lord has a reason for it,' she said. But I wouldn't believe it. There couldn't be any reason for a disappointment like this."

I shifted uncomfortably in my chair, aware that I had thought exactly the same thing just a short time ago. But Grandma seemed not to notice, and went on with her story.

"I dozed off and on through the day, between times feeling very miserable and sorry for myself. Finally, toward evening, the buggy turned into the lane, and Pa and the boys returned from the picnic. As the boys hurried to the barn to take care of the chores, Pa remarked, 'Well, Mabel can be glad she didn't go to the picnic in her nice new dress today.'

17

"Glad! Whatever did he mean? How could I be glad to have missed the big picnic of the year?

"Pa was going on. 'Carter's river is pretty high today, and the children were warned to stay away from it. But the little girls forgot, I guess. They wandered too close and slipped in. The current was so strong that they were carried nearly to the pasture before we could get them out. They were a scared bunch of girls, I'll tell you. They all had to be taken home.'

"Pa looked at me reflectively. 'Your friend, Sarah Jane, ruined her good dress,' he said. 'And you would have been right with her.'

"This was true, I knew. We were always together. And what if we hadn't been pulled out in time? Why, this might have been the last birthday I would have had! As the rest of the family ate supper, I thought about the day and Ma's comment that God had a reason for my staying home. Maybe I did believe it, after all.

"I wore my birthday dress a little late, but whenever I wore it, I was reminded that God orders the lives of His children for their good."

Grandma and I continued to tie the quilt in silence. I was still disappointed about my missed trip, but if, as Grandma said, God knows what is best for His children, maybe I should just be glad that I was one of them! There would be lots of days ahead for trips to the city —and surely there must be a lot more stories in these quilt squares!

3

The Red Bonnet

ONE OF MY FAVORITE squares in Grandma's quilt was a soft red velvet. When I brushed over it with my finger, it seemed to change color. One way was dark, and brushing the other way made it look lighter.

"Grandma," I said, "did you have something made out of this material?"

"Yes," said Grandma. "I was the last in the line to have that. When Ma was married, she brought many things with her to Michigan. One of her most prized possessions was a pair of red velvet drapes. When she and Pa moved into the new log cabin, Ma decided that the drapes wouldn't look especially good at the cabin windows, so they were cut to cover a cushion for Ma's rocker. Another piece made a pretty pin cushion for her sewing basket. The rest of the material was put in the big trunk to be used later when the need arose.

"The winter I was four, Ma brought out the red velvet and made a coat and bonnet for me."

Grandma looked fondly at the soft square.

"It seems as though I can still feel how soft that bonnet and coat were. I wore them for several winters, but the time Ma remembered best was the first time I had them on.

"We lived several miles from the nearest neighbor, and it was often lonely for Ma with just the two boys and me to keep her company during the day. So when Pa came in one evening to announce that there was to be a sing at the Carters' the following Friday, Ma began at once to make plans for the big event. The shoes must be brushed and polished, the boys' clothes put in good order, and I would wear my new coat and bonnet for the first time.

"Everyone was excited about the outing because it was so seldom that we had a chance to meet with the neighbors for a social time.

"When Friday arrived, it was snowing. The ground was covered, and more continued to fall throughout the day. We children were sure that this would put an end to our trip, and we couldn't enjoy the snow as much as we usually did. However, Pa was not to be turned back by a little thing like snow.

" 'I'll hitch the horse to the sleigh,' he told Ma. 'You get some quilts to wrap around the children, and I'll fill the sleigh with straw. They'll be warm enough.'

"So with great excitement we were dressed and wrapped warmly for the trip. The snow had stopped and the stars were beginning to come out when we reached the Carters'. I don't remember much about the evening, aside from hearing the singing and talking, for I went to sleep on Ma's lap before it was time to go home.

"Ma told me later what happened that night that made it so memorable for her. When they were ready to leave, Ma put my coat and bonnet on me, and Pa wrapped me in the big quilt. Then he put me in the sleigh with the boys, where I continued to sleep during the trip home.

"I can remember waking, and seeing a light shining from the cabin door. I climbed out of the sleigh and headed straight for my bed. I slept in a trundle bed that slid under Ma's bed. It was pulled out at night for me, but since we had been away all evening, my bed was not ready. This made no difference to me; I just climbed in with my clothes on and promptly fell asleep again.

"No one had seen me enter the cabin. Roy had gone to shut the gate, Reuben was helping Pa unhitch the horse, and Ma had returned to the front of the sleigh to get the blanket and warming brick she and Pa had used. After putting these things in the cabin, Ma returned to the sleigh to get me.

"She reached into the straw and pulled the quilt toward her. It was empty!

" 'Pa!' she called frantically. 'Pa, Mabel isn't here!'

"Pa ran to the sleigh.

" 'Now, Maryanne,' he said, 'she has to be there. Where else would she be?'

"He climbed into the sleigh and held the lantern high while he looked through the straw. Ma pulled the quilt out and began to shake it, as though she might have overlooked me in the dark. As she did so, my red bonnet fell out on the snow.

" 'Oh, Pa,' she wailed. 'Here's Mabel's bonnet. Now I know we've lost her. She must have fallen out of the sleigh along the road somewhere. We'll have to go back and look for her.'

"The boys stood silently by as Ma continued to shake the quilt, and Pa felt around through the straw.

" 'Didn't you boys watch out for your sister?' he asked them. 'Didn't you see her when she fell out?'

"They shook their heads dumbly, and Roy began to cry. Reuben protested that I couldn't have fallen out, or he surely would have seen me.

"Finally Pa told Ma to get the boys to bed, and he would go back over the road and search for me. When the boys were in bed, Ma began to walk back and forth across the little cabin, clutching my red bonnet, and praying that the Lord would help Pa find me before I froze to death.

"When Pa returned home much later and reported that there was no sign of me, Ma was in despair. Pa had gone back to Carters', and Brother Carter and his boys were joining in the search. With lanterns swinging, the men tramped through the ditches beside the road, calling my name. When they had finally covered all the ground several times they came back to the cabin to decide what was to be done.

"Ma had fixed hot coffee, and they sat around the fire warming their feet and hands before starting out again.

" 'Well,' Pa said, 'we'll just have to trust the Lord to take care of her. I can't imagine where we could have lost her. I know she was in the sleigh when we left for home.'

"About that time I must have awakened and heard voices, for I crawled out from under the big bed to see what was going on. Ma and Pa stared in disbelief when they saw me, still dressed in my red coat, standing in the middle of the cabin. Of course, I had no explanation. I had been sleepy and had gone to bed. It was as simple as that to me. The relieved Carters left for their long ride home, and Ma put me back to bed.

"It was a long time before Ma or Pa could see the funny side of that evening. They made sure it never happened again by keeping me in front with them whenever we went somewhere in the sleigh. But in later years, they laughed about the night I 'fell out of the sleigh' and caused a search party to spend many anxious hours looking for me."

4

Grandpa's Apron

"LOOK HERE, Grandma," I said. "This square is awfully heavy. What was it from?"

Grandma and I were tying her big quilt, and many of the big squares had yielded a good story. Grandma looked, and then a twinkle came to her eye.

"Well, now," she said. "That was a pocket from your Grandpa's apron."

"*Grandpa's* apron! Did Grandpa really have his own apron?" I giggled.

"He certainly did," Grandma laughed. "And you aren't the first one who thought that was funny!"

"Tell me about it, Grandma," I said.

So Grandma began. "Grandpa came home from town one day with this big heavy piece of goods. He said he wanted an apron made for himself—a very special apron. That evening he drew a picture of it for me, and together we cut a pattern out of paper. It was a special apron, too. It had a pocket for everything Grandpa wanted with him.

"There was a pocket to hold Scripture verses, written on cards. These verses were pulled out and recited to Nellie and Bess while Grandpa milked in the morning and at night.

"There was a deeper pocket that held a small song book. It was propped on the stall and Grandpa sang all the verses of 'How Firm A Foundation' or 'O This Uttermost Salvation' to the stock as he fed and watered them.

"Sermon notes were in another pocket. They came out as Grandpa followed behind the plow, and the horses were treated to next Sunday's sermon while they walked up and down the rows.

"One little pocket in a handy place held round, pink wintergreen drops with small x's on them. Another had a selection of nails that often came in handy. There was room for a fresh cooky or a piece of homemade bread and butter. I'm not sure I ever knew what was in all those pockets, but Grandpa did.

"It was a funny-looking apron, to be sure, and Grandpa took a lot of good-natured teasing about it. My brother Reuben would say, 'Here comes Len in his milk-maid's apron. Do you suppose the cows would give any milk if he forgot to wear it?'

"Or Roy would say, 'Oh, Len, do you have an empty pocket in your apron to carry my tools to the back field?'

"Grandpa would laugh along with them, but he would say, 'I hope you boys notice that I don't make a dozen trips to the house or barn while I'm working. I have everything right where I need it.'

"And so Grandpa continued to replenish his pockets and wear this apron as he went about his chores. But a day was to come when no one laughed at Grandpa's apron.

"One afternoon in the fall, Grandpa was working in the hayloft, repairing the floor before the new hay came in. Somehow his foot slipped on a crossbeam, and he

started to fall. His apron flew out and caught on the hook that was used to lift the bales to the loft, and Grandpa hung suspended many feet over the concrete barn floor.

"He began to pray loudly for the Lord to send someone to the barn. The Lord heard him. So did Reuben and Roy, who ran to the barn door to find the reason for such loud prayers.

"Quickly they pushed the hay-wagon under Grandpa and began to lower the haylift, with Grandpa still attached to it, onto the wagon bed.

" 'You boys get me down from here,' Grandpa shouted, 'and maybe I can talk Mabel into making *you* an apron like this!'

"As they loosened the hook from Grandpa's apron, Reuben exclaimed, 'What in the world kept that hook from going clean to the bottom of this silly apron?'

" 'Why, the Lord did, of course,' Grandpa responded. 'And now maybe you clowns will have a little more respect for this valuable piece of goods.'

"He stalked to the house, leaving Reuben and Roy to contemplate the distance that he would have fallen to the barn floor, had not the Lord—and his apron—held him securely.

"I mended the apron, and Grandpa continued to keep it stocked and in use. The boys didn't laugh again. They knew they had seen a miracle that day."

Grandma laughed and patted the square on the quilt.

"That sure was a strong piece of goods," she said. "And you wouldn't be here to listen to the story if your Grandpa hadn't been wearing it that afternoon!"

5

Ma's Busy Day

GRANDMA'S QUILT was almost finished. We had been tying it and talking about the bright-colored squares that had so many good stories in them.

"I'd like a dress like this, Grandma," I said, pointing to a square with tiny green leaves and flowers. "This is pretty."

"Yes," replied Grandma. "That was pretty made up. It was one of Ma's dresses, then she made it into an apron. In fact, a lot of these squares came from Ma's aprons. She was never seen anyplace but in church without an apron on."

Grandma laughed. "Pa never let her forget that she tied an apron over her nightgown one night before she got into bed! I remember another day that Ma didn't live down for a long time, too."

Grandma sat down by the table, and I pulled up the kitchen stool.

"When Ma dressed in the morning," Grandma began, "she put on a clean apron over her housedress. Then she carried a fresh one with her to the kitchen to hang on the back door. This was to make sure that, should we have company, there would be a clean apron in close reach and she would be ready to greet the visitor.

"This morning as usual, Ma hung her extra apron on the door and prepared to fix breakfast. I was setting the table and the boys were coming from the barn with the milk. Ma hurried to open the door and let them in. Pep, our big dog, had also seen them coming and figured this might be a chance to get into the warm kitchen. He lunged for the door just as Roy was going through. One of the milk pails flew into the air, and Roy and Pep were covered with fresh warm milk.

" 'Oh, that dog,' Ma sputtered. 'There's only one thing he can do better than make a mess, and that's eat.'

"She mopped up the milk, sent Roy to change his clothes, and rubbed at the front of her apron with a towel.

" 'I haven't time to change now,' she said, and she grabbed the apron from the door and put it on over the spattered one.

"This was baking day, and Ma was busy making bread, pies and cakes, keeping the stove hot, and cleaning up the kitchen. She had no time to think again about her apron. Shortly before dinner time at noon, Ma saw a buggy turn in the lane.

" 'Mabel,' Ma called to me, 'run and get me a fresh apron, will you? Someone is coming up the lane.'

"I brought the apron, and Ma quickly put it on and tied it just as the visitor approached the house. It was a neighbor to ask Ma if she could come that afternoon to see his wife, who was not feeling too well. Of course Ma could, but wouldn't he stay and have dinner with us first?

"After dinner, when Pa and the boys returned to the field, Ma and I packed a basket to take to the neighbor. As we were about to set out, Ma looked down at her apron.

" 'Mabel,' she said, 'I believe I'd better have a fresh apron before we leave.'

"I got another apron, and Ma tied it on as we walked to the buggy.

"It was getting on toward suppertime when we returned. Ma planned what we would fix, and we hurried about the kitchen getting supper on the table before Pa and the boys should come in.

"As we prepared to sit down, Ma decided that her apron didn't look very good, so she hurried to the bedroom for another.

"Pa came in and sat down at the table. He watched Ma as she finished taking up the food and supervising the boys' washing.

" 'Maryanne,' Pa said, 'have you been putting on weight?'

" 'Why, no,' Ma replied. 'I don't think so. My clothes feel the same. Why?'

" 'Well,' said Pa, 'I declare you look bigger than you did this morning when I left the house.'

" 'I know why,' I said. 'Ma's got more clothes on than she did this morning.'

"Ma looked puzzled for a moment, then she began to laugh.

" 'I guess I have,' she said. 'I've been rushing around so fast today, I haven't had time to take one apron off before I put the other one on.'

"She began to untie the aprons and take them off. With each one Pa and the boys laughed harder. When finally she had gotten down to the original milk-spattered apron, Ma was laughing as hard as the rest of us.

" 'If we couldn't remember what happened all day any other way,' Pa said when he could speak again, 'we could always count on Ma's aprons to bring us up to date!'

"Ma enjoyed the joke, but she declared that she was going to be presentable if it did take five aprons a day to do it—and one on top of the other, too!"

Grandma laughed again at the memory, and we returned to work. Such a wonderful quilt this was! Much better than a magic carpet for carrying us back over the years. Why, we had hardly begun to explore all the stories those squares held. Already I had my eye on several more that I knew would stir Grandma's memory and provide us with another trip into the past.

6

Grandma's Mistake

IT WAS TIME for school to start, and my new plaid dress hung on the door ready for the big day.

"That dress reminds me of my school dress when I was about your age," said Grandma. "Only mine was wool and had long sleeves. Here's a piece of it in the quilt." And Grandma pointed to a plaid square in the quilt folded across my bed.

"You didn't have just one school dress, did you, Grandma?" I asked.

"No," said Grandma. "I had three that year as I remember. We wore pinafores over our dresses then, so we didn't need as many. But I did like that red plaid dress."

"Did you like school when you were little, Grandma?" I asked.

"Oh, yes," Grandma replied. "I couldn't wait to get to school. It did start out as a big disappointment, though." Grandma laughed and picked up her mending beside the rocker. I could see a story coming, so I pulled up my little chair and sat down.

"Ma had taught me my letters and how to sound out a few words before I started school," Grandma began. "I was so anxious to read that I would sit with the boys' school books and try to pick out words I knew. I think the whole family was glad when I was finally old enough to go to school and they weren't being pestered to tell me what the words were.

"The little school we went to was a one-room school that had all eight grades together. Sometimes there would only be one or two children in a grade. The beginners sat in front, and each grade was arranged in order, with the big boys and girls in the back. The classes came to the benches around the blackboard to recite. I had a seat with my special friend, Sarah Jane, in the beginners' row. We did our letters and numbers together, and also spent a lot of time listening to the other boys and girls as they would come to the front.

"One day, while the second reader class was reciting, the teacher called on Billy to read a sentence from the board. Billy was older than the others in his class, because he had repeated the first reader. We children thought he was just dumb, but that wasn't the reason. He had been sick most of the winter, and missed a lot of school. Of course, Billy was embarrassed about being the biggest boy in his class. He stood to read the sentence, but he didn't know all the words. Since I had been listening to the class, I read it for him.

"Billy sat down, red-faced and unhappy. The older children tittered. I felt rather proud of myself for having known more than Billy did, and even when the teacher said, 'That's fine, Mabel, but you finish your letters now,' I still felt a little bigger than the other beginners.

"My pride was not to last long, however. Reuben reported what had happened to Ma.

" 'Mabel is acting too smart in school, Ma,' he said. 'She made Billy feel like a fool today. She acts like she knows it all.'

"I tossed my head defiantly. 'Well, I did know the words, and Billy didn't,' I said proudly.

" 'Reuben is right, Mabel,' said Ma. 'You've no business showing off in front of the school. You made Billy feel bad by reading for him.'

"I hung my head. I hadn't thought I was doing anything wrong.

" 'After this,' said Ma, 'you are not to speak up, even if you do know the answer. It's not ladylike to act so smart. Do you understand?'

"I nodded my head. I understood that if I knew something, I was to keep it to myself. I also understood that Reuben and Roy would be watching out for me, and any slip would be reported to Ma.

"The teacher boarded around at different homes during the school year. Her first place was the minister's home. Toward the middle of the first term, she happened to remark to the minister's wife, 'I thought Mabel O'Dell was going to be a bright student. But I guess I was mistaken. She doesn't say anything at all in school. When I call on her, she just shakes her head and ducks behind her book. I can't understand it.'

"Ma couldn't understand it either, when this news was passed on to her. She had heard me reading my book at home, and the boys drilled me on my sums until I knew them well. She approached the subject at supper time.

" 'Mabel, are you having trouble at school?' she asked.

" 'No, Ma,' I replied. 'I get along fine.'

" 'Can you read your lessons every day?'

" 'Sure, Ma. I can read the whole book!'

"Ma was puzzled. 'Then why,' she asked, 'does the teacher say you don't recite in school?'

"I was surprised. 'Why, Ma,' I answered, 'you told me not to!'

" 'I told you not to!' Ma exclaimed. 'Why, Mabel, I did no such thing!'

" 'Yes, Ma, you did,' I said. 'You told me not to speak up, even when I knew the answer. Don't you remember?'

"Ma remembered. Even though she was annoyed with me for not knowing the difference between reciting for myself or for someone else, she had to laugh. The matter was soon straightened out, and my schoolwork improved. If it hadn't been for the minister's wife, school would have been a big disappointment for me!"

7

The Button Basket

OF ALL THE THINGS in Grandma's house that could delight a little girl, there was nothing that even approached the button basket. It sat high on the old china cabinet and was brought down on special occasions of confinement to bed, or possibly to soothe a severe case of disappointment. The basket looked rather ordinary from the floor. It was almost a foot in diameter and was tightly woven of dark brown reeds. But when one looked at the top, it was far from ordinary! Bright-colored beads were sewed in an unusual pattern. Some of the beads flopped when I ran my fingers over them, for the basket was old. Almost as old as Grandma, in fact.

"Where did you get the basket, Grandma?" I asked one day. "Did your mother buy it for you?"

"Oh, no," Grandma replied. "I should say not. That basket came in an unusual way."

Grandma looked fondly at the basket and continued her story.

"I was only five years old when it all happened, but I can remember very clearly that summer day. We lived in a new log house that Pa had just finished way up in the northern woods of Michigan. Our nearest neighbors were more than five miles away, and we seldom had company. Although the man from whom Pa bought the land had assured Pa that the Indians thereabouts were friendly, we still had a fear of meeting one of them, and never ran beyond the clearing without either Ma or Pa with us.

"On this morning, Pa had left at dawn for the long drive into town for supplies. Ma had assured him that we would be all right alone. The boys were big (Reuben was eight and Roy was almost seven), and they would look after us women folks.

"The day was fine and warm, and the boys had hurried through their chores and were playing a game with sticks and pine cones. I was swinging in the rope swing Pa had hung for me in the tree nearest the cabin. Ma was singing as she worked, and the boys were shouting, so it was not strange that no one heard when someone approached the cabin from the woods.

"Suddenly, it seemed too quiet. The boys were standing still and open-mouthed. Ma had stopped singing and was staring toward the woods beyond the clearing. For there, slowly and softly, came a tall Indian toward us.

"'Children, come here,' Ma called, and we quickly ran to hide behind her skirts.

"'Now don't make any noise,' she warned. 'We don't want to scare him. Maybe he's lost or something.'

"She knew, of course, that he was not. Indians did not get lost in their own woods. She just needed to reassure herself as well as us.

"The Indian was taller than anyone I had ever seen. Much taller than Pa. He wore buckskin trousers and had bright beads around his neck. His hair was in a long braid, and more beads were woven through the braid.

He stood straight and broad-shouldered in front of Ma and held out his hand. Ma shrank back against the cabin, and I began to cry in terror.

"It was Reuben who noticed that the Indian carried a brown basket. He held it toward Ma, as though wanting her to take it.

" 'It's a peace offering, Ma,' said Reuben. 'He wants you to have it.'

"Timidly, Ma reached out and took the basket. The Indian stood, watching her. Ma knew that she must give something in return, but what did she have? Quickly she turned and ran into the cabin and looked about frantically for something to offer the Indian.

" 'I'll get something shiny,' she thought, and reached for the pewter cups she had brought from home. The Indian, however, shook his head. Ma offered him the only mirror we owned. He looked at it curiously, then handed it back with another shake of his head.

"What did he want? How could she find out? The Indian stood in the doorway, his eyes taking in every detail of the little one-room cabin. Then he walked to the stove and uncovered the loaves of fresh bread that had just come from the oven. Food! Of course, that was it. As quickly as she could, Ma wrapped the loaves in a towel and thrust them at the Indian. We children watched wide-eyed as she added the remainder of our sugar supply, several cans of fruit, and the pie she had made for Pa's supper.

"The Indian seemed pleased. He now held all he could possibly carry, and without a sound he turned and left the little cabin. We watched as he crossed the clearing with his bounty, and then Ma sank weakly to the doorstep as he disappeared quietly into the woods.

"We did not venture away from the cabin again that day, and all of us were much relieved to see Pa returning in the buggy as twilight fell. Everyone tried at one time to tell Pa what had happened. The basket was quite forgotten until Pa saw it lying on the bed where Ma had dropped it.

"He picked it up and studied it carefully. 'This is a beautiful piece of handiwork,' he said. 'It is hand-woven, and those beads would tell an Indian legend if we knew how to read them. I'd like to know the story.'

" 'Well, I've had enough story for one day,' replied Ma. 'You can just put that basket away until I get my breath back and my heart is in place again.'

"So the basket was put away. Eventually, however, Ma decided it would make a good sewing basket, so it was put to use. She insisted, however, that she didn't care enough about the story to want the Indian to come back and tell it to her!"

8

Little Gray Shoes

THE WINTER I was six years old, I had diphtheria. After a few weeks, when I began to feel a little better, Grandma brought the basket to my bed. Most everything in Grandma's house had a story, but the basket was full of them!

The basket contained buttons . . . all sizes, shapes, colors, and kinds. There were so many things to do with them, that it was hard to know how to start. Should I sort out all the round buttons? Or string the red buttons all together? Or maybe see how many different shapes there were? I seemed never to get to the end of the possibilities.

On this day, as I dug to the bottom of the basket, my fingers felt a new shape—one I hadn't noticed before. I brought the button out and looked at it curiously. It was a small silver-grey triangle. It had no holes through it, nor a hook on the back. There seemed to be no way to sew it on anything.

"Grandma," I called. "Here's a button I never saw before. Where did it come from?"

Grandma came to look. She turned the button over in her hand thoughtfully.

"Why, this was one of my shoe buttons," she replied.

"Shoe button?" I asked. "Did you wear shoes with buttons on them? How was the button fastened on?"

"Oh, yes," said Grandma, "my shoes had buttons all the way up the side. The little hook that held this button came off long ago. I guess this is the only one that hasn't been lost."

Grandma continued to turn the button over in her hand. Her eye had the faraway look of a story, so I settled back on the pillows and waited.

"These were the most beautiful shoes I had ever seen," Grandma began. "We only had one new pair a year, and it was very important to make a good choice. Ma took me into town in September to shop for my new shoes. The first pair the man brought out were these wonderful gray shoes with silver triangle buttons. They were soft doe-skin, and to me, there had never been anything so lovely.

" 'Oh, Ma,' I said. 'These are the ones I want.' I don't even want to look at any others.'

" 'Well, try them on,' said Ma. 'We'll see.'

"The man put the shoes on my feet and buttoned them up with a tiny buttonhook. I held my feet straight out in front of me and admired those shoes. Oh, such beauty!

" 'Stand up,' said Ma. 'See if they are going to be too short.'

"Too short! Of course they weren't. They couldn't be. But when I stood down on the floor, my toes touched the end of the shoes.

" 'Do they pinch?' asked the man.

" 'Oh, no, they don't pinch! They are just fine!' I hastened to reassure them.

"But Ma was doubtful.

" 'Remember,' she said. 'You have to wear these all year. It doesn't look like there is much room to grow. Do you have them in the next size?' she asked.

"He didn't. All he had in the next size was a pair of black shoes with shiny patent leather toes and small round buttons. The thought of leaving those wonderful gray shoes was more than I could stand.

" 'These are just fine, Ma,' I protested. 'These fit just fine. They don't hurt a bit.'

"A little twinge told me that the shoes really were too small, and that I should tell Ma that my toes touched the end. But my desire to have a beautiful pair of shoes to show Sarah Jane and the other girls won out, and I said nothing.

"Ma paid for the shoes, and they were wrapped for me to carry home in triumph. I wore them to church the following Sunday, and modestly accepted the admiration of my friends.

"For a few weeks, the shoes only felt a little tight. Then as my feet continued to grow, they really began to pinch. Of course, I could say nothing to Ma. I could not admit that I had stretched the truth to get them, and anyway, there was no money to replace them. Finally I found that I could only wear the shoes when I was sitting down, so that I could curl my toes up inside. On Sunday morning, I would pull my boots on over my heavy stockings and carefully conceal my shoes under my cape until we got to church. Then I would sit through the long service with my poor feet aching in those beautiful shoes.

"The day came, as I knew it would, when I could not get the shoes on at all. Ma had to be told. With much sobbing, I admitted that I had been deceitful about the shoes. Now it was only early in December, and I had no shoes to wear for the remainder of the winter.

"Ma was sorry, not only that the shoes no longer fit, but that her little girl had deceived her. Oh, what I

would have given for those homely black shoes that would fit! But that was impossible. There was no money for more shoes. The only solution was a pair of my older brother's outgrown shoes.

"Pa tried his best to shine them up for me, but they were boy's shoes! And they had metal toes! I would never leave the house again. I would just stay home until it was time to go barefoot in the spring. But of course I didn't. Although I cried huge tears over them, I wore Roy's shoes to church. I did my best to hide my feet under the bench so no one would see, but such things are not easy to hide.

"When Christmas came, I was delighted to see among my gifts a new rag doll that Ma had made and wrapped in a knitted shawl. But when I pulled back the shawl, what should look up at me but two gray shoe-button eyes! I looked quickly at Ma, but she acted as though nothing was wrong. I looked again at the doll. Her smiling mouth was not really laughing at me, I decided. In fact, she looked quite sympathetic. I touched the little buttons and thought how foolish I had been. This little doll would remind me to think twice before I did a deceitful thing like that again!

"My gray-eyed Emily was my companion until I was too old for dolls. There were others, even one with a china head, but none so dear as Emily with her kind smile and shoe-button eyes."

Grandma dropped the button into the basket and went back to her work. I dozed off thinking of the little gray shoes, and Grandma, a little girl just like me.

9

Nellie and the Buttons

"Look, Grandma," I said, "here are six buttons just alike, and they look like they've been chewed. What were these on?"

I had been in bed a long time recovering from diphtheria, and Grandma had given me the basket to keep me company. Since the basket was full of buttons of all shapes and sizes, I never ran out of entertainment.

Grandma had been working by the window, but now she came to the bed where the buttons were spread out.

"Those were my coat buttons, and they *were* chewed," she said. "Since I was the only girl in our family until I was almost grown up, I never had to wear hand-me-down dresses as some of my friends did. Ma made all our clothes, even Pa's and the boys'. But if I did have my own dresses, my coats were nearly always cut down from the boys' coats when they were outgrown.

"This winter, Reuben needed a new coat, but Roy did not, so Ma decided to make my winter coat out of Reuben's old one. He was growing so tall that he had only worn it one year, and the wool was still good.

"Ma took it apart carefully, cleaned and brushed the pieces, and soon there was a nice new coat for me. I liked the coat very much, but I did want new buttons on it. Ma thought not. These were good buttons and would look fine just as they had on Reuben's coat.

" 'But Ma,' I protested, 'everyone will know that was Reuben's coat with those old buttons on it. Why can't I just have some pretty new ones? They don't cost much.'

"Pa was sympathetic and offered to go to town for buttons, but Ma would not hear of it. We didn't need to spend money for something that wasn't necessary.

"When Ma had her mind made up, there was no point in wasting time trying to change it. So I resigned myself to the old buttons and began to be anxious for the weather to turn cold so I could wear the coat.

"When it did get cold, though, we discovered something that no one had counted on.

"Reuben was the oldest boy, and since he had been small, he had followed Pa about the farm and tried to help. He was personally acquainted with every animal on the place, and they were all close friends. Whenever Reuben went to the barn or field, the horses, cows, pigs, and sheep came to be talked to and rubbed. Reuben had named each one, and seemed to have time to give them all some attention. Pa had grumbled about farm animals not being pets, but no one thought seriously of stopping Reuben, for he did have a way with animals. His special friend was Nellie, a horse he had raised from a colt.

"One evening Ma said to me, 'Mabel, put on your coat and run out to the barn. Ask Pa to bring some eggs when he comes in.'

"I hurried quickly across the frosty yard to deliver the message. I, too, had been a frequent visitor to the barn, but I wasn't old enough yet to help with the animals, and they never paid much attention to me. This evening, however, was different. Just outside the barn door stood Nellie. Before I could enter, she had banged her head against my stomach, and I sat down hard.

"Reuben came running when he heard me scream, and led Nellie away from the door. When he had picked me up and brushed me off, he said to Pa, 'Whatever got into that horse? She's never done that before.'

" 'I guess Mabel startled her, running up like that,' replied Pa. 'I don't think Nellie meant to hurt her.'

"Nevertheless, when I went to the barn the next morning, I was careful to walk a long way around Nellie. I needn't have bothered. She didn't even notice me.

"The following Sunday, Reuben hitched Nellie to the buggy for our trip to church. Of course I was wearing my new coat, and as I walked in front of the horse to get in the buggy, Nellie reached out again and butted me with her head. This time, before Pa could reach me, Nellie was chewing on one of my coat buttons.

" 'Now what did she do that for?' asked Ma. 'What's the matter with that horse, anyway? Mabel, have you been teasing her?'

"No, I had not. In fact, I had been going out of my way to stay away from her. There seemed to be no reason for a gentle horse to suddenly begin knocking a little girl around.

"The odd thing was that Nellie didn't do it every time she saw me. Most of the time she paid no attention to me at all. Finally, after several encounters when the horse had managed to chew my coat buttons before someone could rescue me, Reuben came up with the answer.

" 'Ma,' he said, 'Nellie only goes after Mabel when she has that coat on. I think Nellie remembers those buttons when they were on my coat. I trained her to shake the front of my coat to get sugar. I think that's what she wants, and she isn't just knocking Mabel down to be mean.'

"But Ma was doubtful.

" 'I know you think that horse is pretty smart,' she told Reuben, 'but she isn't smart enough to remember buttons.'

"However, when Nellie continued to make life miserable for me whenever I wore that coat, Ma began to change her mind. Finally one day she said to Pa, 'I believe Reuben is right about that coat. Maybe I'd better change the buttons and see if Nellie will leave Mabel alone.'

"So I had my wish after all. Pa and I made the trip to town and picked out new buttons for my coat. And sure enough, Nellie didn't do any more than look at me when I walked past her. The old buttons went into Ma's sewing basket, and Reuben bragged to his friends about the smart horse he had."

Grandma returned to her work, and I examined the buttons closely, trying to imagine Grandma as a little girl, having her buttons chewed by a smart horse!

10

The Pearl Buttons

GRANDMA AND I were eating lunch.

"There's a button missing from your sweater," said Grandma. "Do you know where it is?"

"No, Grandma," I said. "I must have lost it on the playground or someplace."

"Go fetch me the button basket," said Grandma. "Maybe I can match it."

I ran to get the basket. Together we looked through the buttons for one that would fit my sweater. Grandma found it, and while she sewed it on, I stirred the buttons around with my finger. I had looked at them all so many times, but I never tired of playing with them or hearing stories about them.

"I think these little pearl buttons are nice, Grandma," I said. I had picked out eight of them and laid them in a row on the table.

"How many are there?"

"There used to be fifteen of them," said Grandma. "I don't know whether they are all there now or not."

"What had that many buttons on it?" I asked.

"My new dress for the school program," Grandma laughed. "And Ma wished she had never put them on it before the evening was over!"

"Why, Grandma?" I asked. "Tell me what happened."

"It's time for you to get back to school," Grandma said. "Leave the buttons there. I'll tell you about it this afternoon."

When school was out, I hurried home to hear the story. Grandma was taking bread out of the oven, and she cut a crust for me to eat.

"The dress was a pretty blue," Grandma began. "Ma had made it especially for the end of the year program at school. Everyone in the school had a piece to say or a song to sing. The families all came to the school in the evening, and after the program there was ice cream and cake for everyone. It was one of the biggest events of the year. I had been saying my piece over so many times that Pa teased me about it.

" 'If you decide you don't want to go to the program, I can say your piece for you,' he said.

" 'Maybe you could say my piece,' I said, 'but you couldn't wear my new dress. And that's the most important part.'

" 'Now Mabel,' said Ma, 'you shouldn't be so proud. Nobody is going to pay near as much attention to your dress as they will to how well you speak.'

"Poor Ma didn't know how wrong she was that time.

"The dress had a nice big pocket on the skirt and fifteen buttons that fastened down the back. Ma had crocheted little loops to fasten them. I thought they looked especially pretty, but I didn't say any more about the dress.

"When the evening of the program arrived, everyone was in a hurry to get ready. It seemed that everything happened to slow us down. It was about time to leave, and Ma had not changed her clothes yet. I had finished dressing, all but fastening the buttons on my dress, which I couldn't do. When I went to Ma to be buttoned, she said, 'Ask Pa to do it, Mabel. I've got to get dressed too.' But Pa had another trip to the barn before we left.

"'Get one of your brothers to help you,' he said. 'I couldn't fasten those little buttons anyway.'

"I knew better than to ask Reuben or Roy to button my dress. I'd just have to wait for Ma. But Ma took so long getting ready that I heard Pa bring Nellie and the buggy around. There was nothing to do but help myself. I certainly didn't want them to go off and leave me. I quickly took off the dress, turned it around, and fastened the buttons up the front.

"Pa was calling for us to hurry, so I slipped into my coat and ran to the buggy. We arrived at the school on time, and I hurried to join my friends in the front row. The school was crowded and didn't look at all like the place we had come every day to work.

"It was soon time for the program to begin. The younger children were the first to recite, so I was near the beginning. I could hardly wait for my turn to come. Finally my name was called. I took off my coat and marched proudly to the platform. Behind me I heard giggles and whispers. I turned around to see what could be the matter.

"The older people were trying not to smile, but the children were laughing openly. And they were laughing at me! I looked around to see what I had done. I could see nothing funny. I looked at Ma, but she had her head down. Pa was shaking with laughter. Then I heard one of the girls in the front.

"'Look at that!' she said. 'Mabel has her dress on backwards!'

"I looked down at the neat row of buttons. I didn't think that looked so bad. Then I remembered. That big pocket was on the back! No one but boys had pockets on the back of their clothes! The evening was ruined for me. I mumbled my piece and sat down again, red-faced and humiliated.

"I don't remember hearing much of the program. Even when the teacher assured me that I had done just fine, my spirits didn't lift much. The ice cream and cake weren't nearly as good as they should have been, and it was awfully warm in the school with a coat on. But I wouldn't take it off, no matter how warm I got!

"To my relief, Pa was ready to leave early. I was more than glad to climb into the buggy and start for home. Of course Roy had to say something about my disgrace.

" 'That's just like a girl,' he said. 'She would have to do something silly so people would notice her.'

"But Ma was sympathetic. 'Now don't tease your sister,' she said. 'She didn't do it on purpose. We were just all too busy to help her, that's all. It's too bad I didn't notice before we left.'

"Pa chuckled. 'But she did look like she had her head screwed on backwards when she walked up there,' he said.

" 'Now, Pa, you're as bad as the boys,' Ma scolded. 'Mabel feels bad enough already. Don't make her feel worse!'

"Of course I got over it all right. But that dress was never quite the same again. Though no one mentioned it, I was sure they all remembered how funny I had looked whenever I wore the dress to church. Ma didn't make a dress with so many buttons on the back again. And she was careful to check on me before we left the house to go somewhere."

Grandma laughed at the memory.

"It seems funny now," she said, "but it was far from funny then. I guess it was just what I needed to take me down a peg."

11

Nellie's Trips to Town

THE RAIN WAS splashing down, and I was bored.

"Grandma," I said, "what did you do to have fun when you were a little girl?"

"Oh, my," said Grandma. "There was lots to do on the farm. We had a swing in the big tree. We played in the barn loft when it rained. We waded in the brook and picked berries and nuts. There was always something to keep us busy."

"Didn't you ever go away on any trips?" I asked. "Did you have to stay on the farm all the time?"

"We went to church on Sunday," said Grandma. "And sometimes we went to town with Ma and Pa for the day. That was a big treat."

Grandma worked on her crocheting a few moments. Then she chuckled and said, "I remember one trip to town that had a funny ending. Run and get me another ball of thread, and I'll tell you about it."

I hurried back with the thread, and Grandma began the story.

"It was a Friday, I remember. Pa had several errands in town, and Ma wanted to do some shopping. So it was decided that the whole family would go and make a day of it. The boys hurried through their chores while Ma and I packed a lunch to take along. We were soon ready and on our way.

"I went with Ma to pick out dress goods and other things she needed, and the boys went with Pa. We were to meet at the buggy later in the afternoon to get our lunch. We were going to picnic in the little grove at the edge of town. Pa tied Nellie to a hitching post near the blacksmith's shop, and we all went our separate ways.

"Ma and I took a long time picking out material and buttons and thread. Of course there were other things to look at, too. By the time we got back to the blacksmith shop, Pa and the boys were already there.

"Pa was looking up the road with a puzzled expression, and the boys were running around the back of the shop. Nellie and the buggy were nowhere to be seen.

"Ma wasted no time in coming to the point.

" 'Pa,' she said, 'where is Nellie?'

" 'I don't just know,' Pa replied. 'But she doesn't appear to be here.'

" 'Did you tie her tight?' Ma asked. 'Could she have slipped the reins off the post and gone on home?'

" 'That's not likely,' said Pa. 'I'm sure I tied her as tight as usual. There must be some explanation for this.'

" 'Well,' said Ma. 'I wish you'd find it in a hurry. Our lunch is in the buggy, and it's getting late.'

" 'Yes, Pa,' I said. 'I'm hungry.'

" 'We'll find Nellie, all right,' said Pa. 'Don't worry. I'll ask around and see if anyone saw her start away.'

"No one had. The blacksmith had noticed several buggies come and go, but he couldn't say who was in them. There were still several horses tied there, but none of them was Nellie. Anyone who had noticed a horse pulling an empty buggy would surely have stopped it.

"Evening was coming on, and we children were getting hungrier, Ma was getting more worried, and Pa had exhausted all the possibilities he could think of. At last he suggested that we go to the minister's house to rest and decide what to do.

"The minister's wife was surprised to see us, but very hospitable.

" 'Why, of course you'll stay here,' she said, when she had heard the story. 'And after supper, Will can take you out to your place. I'm sure your horse must have gone on home.'

"We were glad she had mentioned supper. The thought of the long ride home with nothing to eat was not a pleasant one for us children. The women began to prepare the meal, and Pa and the minister discussed our problem. There was never any thought that Nellie had been stolen. People just did not steal horses and buggies in our little town. Perhaps some mischievous boys had untied the horse, but even that didn't seem likely with people around all the time.

"There seemed to be no more to do about it that night, so after supper the minister hitched up his buggy, and we got in for our trip home. It was dark now, and only a few people were left on the street. Light shone from the blacksmith shop, however, and as we approached it, Roy called out, 'Look, Pa! There's Nellie, right where we left her!'

"The minister stopped the horse, and Pa jumped down. Sure enough, there was Nellie and the buggy. Pa walked around and looked at the horse in disbelief. Nellie looked back at him as if to say, 'Well, where have you been? Don't you know it's dark?'

"By this time, the rest of us were gathered around. The lunch still sat in the buggy, untouched. We were too astonished to speak.

"Finally Pa said, 'I guess we might as well go home. She's not going to tell us where she's been.'

"He thanked the minister for his help, and we climbed into our own buggy. The trip home was spent trying to find a reasonable explanation for what had happened. We could think of none. Pa was just glad to have the horse and buggy back and be on the way home.

"Saturday morning we were still talking about the mystery when our neighbor, Ed Hobbs, drove into the yard. Pa went out to meet him, and invited him in to breakfast.

" 'Thanks,' said Ed, 'but I've already eaten. I just came to tell you folks what happened yesterday.'

"He sat down at the table and told us the story.

" 'I was pretty busy yesterday,' he said, 'and I had a broken plow that needed to be fixed. I couldn't spare my boy to take it into town, so Grandpa said he'd do it for me. Grandpa's getting pretty old, and doesn't see very well, but I thought he could probably make it to the blacksmith shop all right, so I loaded the plow in the buggy, and Grandpa started out.

" 'It wasn't until early evening, long after Grandpa had returned, that I noticed a strange horse in the barn. Then I saw the buggy out beside the shed. I went into the house to see who was visiting. Grandpa was dozing by the fire, and there was no one else in the kitchen but the family.

" ' "Grandpa," I said, "whose horse is that in the barn?"

" ' "Why, it's our horse, naturally," said Grandpa. "Whose did you think it was?"

" ' "That's not our horse, Grandpa," I said. "It looks like Brother O'Dell's horse and buggy to me."

" ' "Brother O'Dell?" said Grandpa. "Is Brother O'Dell here? Why didn't he come in and sit a spell?"

" ' "No, Grandpa," I replied. "Brother O'Dell isn't here. I think you brought his horse and buggy home."

" ' "Now why would I do a thing like that?" asked Grandpa indignantly. "I wasn't anywhere near the O'Dells' place today!"

" 'I gave up on Grandpa,' said Ed. 'I hitched up your horse and drove it into town. There was our horse and buggy, right in front of the blacksmith shop. The blacksmith said you had been looking for your horse, but he didn't know where you had gone, so I tied her up and came on home. I figured I'd come and tell you about it first thing this morning. I'm sorry about Grandpa. I won't send him on any more errands into town!'

"Pa laughed as hard as we children did. He assured Ed that everything had turned out all right, and Grandpa Hobbs was forgiven. We seldom made a trip to town after that but someone would say, 'Remember when Grandpa Hobbs took Nellie home by mistake?' I guess that was the most memorable trip to town we had when I was a little girl."

Grandma continued to rock and crochet, and I returned to the window to watch the rain, and think what fun it would have been to be a little girl when Grandma was.

12

The New Pump

"BE CAREFUL," said Grandma. "That's hot!"

But I had already taken a swallow of the cocoa, and now I knew it was hot. It burned my tongue, and all the way down.

"That's too bad," said Grandma. "I know how that feels. I've burned my tongue many times. Did you know that something doesn't have to be hot to burn your tongue?"

"You can't burn it on something cold," I said, still rubbing at the tears that had come to my eyes.

"Oh, my," Grandma replied. "You surely can. And much worse than you've just burned yours, too. I know, because I did it once."

"How, Grandma?" I asked.

"I was quite often a foolish little girl," said Grandma. "If someone told me not to do something, that was exactly what I wanted to do. Most of the time I had to pay dearly for it, too. But this time I learned a lesson I didn't forget for a long time.

"It was in the fall that Pa had gotten a new pump. We had drawn the water from a well before, and the pump was a wonderful thing. You just had to move the handle up and down, and the water came gushing out. We all felt quite privileged to have such a wonderful thing in our own yard. The boys didn't fuss about whose turn it was to get water for Ma, and they could fill the horse trough in just a few minutes. The whole family enjoyed that pump.

"The weather had gotten cold early that year, and we had frost 'most every night in October. By November, the snow was falling and the boys needed mittens on when they went to get water in the morning. The well was deep, so the water didn't freeze in the winter. Sometimes the pump would be frozen though, and they would have to bring hot water from the kitchen to pour in and thaw it. Even that extra work didn't take away the enjoyment we children had in that new pump.

"One evening our neighbor, Mr. Hobbs, stopped by to visit. He and Pa sat in the kitchen talking about the crops and the cold weather. I was helping Ma with the dishes. I was always anxious to enter into the conversation, but since I didn't know much about crops, there seemed to be nothing for me to say. However, during a lull in the talking, I thought of something I did know about.

" 'Mr. Hobbs,' I said, 'did you know we have a new pump?'

" 'No,' said Mr. Hobbs. 'Do you really, now? I suppose you bring in all the water for your Ma and water the animals too, don't you?'

"I knew Mr. Hobbs was just teasing. The handle was too heavy for me to move fast enough to get the water started. The boys had let me help them pump sometimes when they were in a good mood. But I laughed along with Mr. Hobbs and Pa. A few minutes later, Mr. Hobbs rose to leave. As he opened the door, he turned to me and said with a laugh, 'Well, Mabel, don't put your tongue on the pump handle!' Then he and Pa went out into the yard.

"That seemed a strange thing to say. Why would I want to do that? I concluded that Mr. Hobbs was teasing again, and thought no more about it.

"Several days later I came out of the house to find everything covered with new snow. I could see my breath in the frosty air, and there were little thin pieces of ice around the edges of the horse trough. I gave the pump handle a few pulls to see if I might be able to get some water, but of course nothing happened. The handle was white with frost, and as I stood looking at it, I remembered Mr. Hobbs' remark. Since he was only fooling, there was no reason why I shouldn't lick the frost off the handle if I wanted to. So I bent over and put my tongue on the pump handle. I knew right away that Mr. Hobbs hadn't been fooling. My tongue was stuck fast!

"It's not very easy to holler without moving your tongue, but I could still cry, and I began to do so. Big tears ran down my cheeks and dripped on the pump handle. Fortunately, Reuben was coming from the barn and saw me.

" 'Mabel, what in the world are you doing?' he asked. Then he saw the predicament I was in.

" 'Wait right here,' he said, 'I'll go get Ma.'

"Of course there was nothing I could do except wait right there, but it was comforting to know that help was on the way.

" 'Ma,' Reuben called, 'Mabel has her tongue stuck on the pump handle!'

"Ma came running out to look.

" 'Don't pull on it, Mabel,' she said. 'Just stay right here and I'll get some warm water.'

"I was getting a little tired of being told to stay right there when they all knew I couldn't possibly move, but I nodded my head the best I could. Ma was soon back with a dipper of warm water.

" 'Now this will hurt,' she said, 'but it's the only way to get your tongue loose. My, what a silly thing for you to do. Didn't you know that anything wet sticks to cold metal?'

"I hadn't known, but I did now. The warm water loosened my tongue, but some of the skin came off too. I'll tell you, I had a sore tongue for a long time. The new pump didn't seem quite as enchanting to me for awhile. I begged Pa not to tell Mr. Hobbs what I had done, and he promised me that no one would hear about it. Ma warned the boys not to tease me; she figured I had suffered enough for my foolishness."

Grandma shook her head at the memory.

"We all have to learn some way," she said, "but I'm sure there's a better way than that to do it. Sometimes we act the same way with God—He tells us not to do things, but we try them anyway. By the time we're sorry about it, we've been hurt and feel just a little foolish."

I slowly finished my cocoa while I thought about Grandma's story.

13

You Can't Always Believe

GRANDMA CALLED ME in from the yard.

"I thought I asked you to put these slippers away," she said.

"But I did, Grandma," I replied. "I put them away when you told me to."

"Then how did they get back out here?" asked Grandma. "You shouldn't say you have done something when you haven't. Now put them away, please."

I picked up the slippers and walked slowly to my room. I *had* put them away when she told me to, and she didn't believe me.

Later that morning, I sat in the big kitchen waiting for the cookies to come out of the oven. Suddenly, around the corner came Skip, the old farm dog, dragging one of my slippers!

"Look, Grandma!" I said. "There's how my slippers got back out here!"

"Well," Grandma said to Skip, "I ought to use that slipper on you. Someone else got the scolding that you deserved.

"I'm sorry, child, that I didn't believe you," she said to me. "Next time I won't be so quick to blame you until I find out what happened."

Grandma took the cookies from the oven, and as she poured a glass of milk for me, she chuckled.

"I remember how something like that happened to my brother Roy," she said. "It wasn't very funny at the time, at least not to Roy, but we have laughed about it since."

"Tell me about it, Grandma," I said.

Grandma slid another pan of cookies into the oven, then sat down at the table.

"It happened when Roy was about ten years old," she began. "It had rained all day Saturday, and into the night. Sunday morning Pa called to Roy, who slept up in the loft above the kitchen with Reuben.

" 'Roy,' Pa said, 'I think I told you to clean your shoes last night before you went to bed.'

" 'I did clean them, Pa,' he said. 'I put them right by the fireplace.'

" 'Well,' said Pa, 'they are by the fireplace all right, but they certainly aren't clean!'

"Roy scrambled down the ladder and stared at the muddy shoes in disbelief.

" 'But, Pa . . .' he began.

" 'Don't "but, Pa," me. Get those shoes cleaned and be quick about it,' said Pa.

"Roy cleaned the shoes, but the look on his face said that something was unfair.

"A few days later, Pa came in from the barn as we were getting ready for school.

" 'Boys,' he asked, 'who was responsible for closing the gate on the sheep pen last night?'

" 'I was, Pa,' answered Roy. 'And I closed it tight. I made sure it was latched.'

" 'Well,' said Pa, 'you can also make sure that the sheep are all back in the pen before you leave for school. The gate was wide open this morning.'

"After Roy had left to take care of the sheep, Pa said, 'That boy needs working on. He doesn't know what responsibility is anymore.'

"On Saturday morning, Ma went up to the boys' room to change the bedding. Under Roy's pillow she found several crumbled cookies and an apple. At noon, when we sat down to eat dinner, Ma said, 'Roy, do you get enough to eat at the table?'

" 'Why, sure, Ma,' Roy said, 'I get plenty to eat.' He looked at her in surprise.

" 'Then why do you take food to bed with you?' Ma asked.

" 'To bed!' said Roy. 'I don't take food to bed!'

" 'Then I suppose Pep put the apple and cookies under your pillow,' Ma replied tartly.

"Roy's mouth dropped open, but before he could say anything, Pa put down his fork and looked sternly across the table.

" 'Young man, it seems that nothing that happens around here is your fault. Now if you don't straighten up and stop this foolishness, I'm going to have to take the strap to you.'

"Roy might have gotten that strapping, too, except that quite by accident I helped him out. I developed a bad case of the croup, and Ma had to get up in the night to fix hot cloths and cough medicine for me. As she stood by the stove, she saw Roy coming down from the loft. He went to the fireplace, put on his shoes and started for the door. Ma was about to call to him when she realized that Roy was fast asleep!

"The moon was full, and the yard was as bright as day. Ma watched as Roy crossed the yard, opened the barn door, and disappeared inside. Before she could call Pa to go get him, Roy reappeared, carrying Nellie's harness. He hung it over the fence, came back to the house, took off his shoes, and went back to bed!

"Roy was as surprised as the rest of us to learn that he had been walking in his sleep. Of course Pa was sorry that he had scolded Roy for things he didn't know he was doing. Ma put an end to the sleepwalking by moving Reuben's bed over the loft opening so that Roy couldn't get down.

"Poor Roy. He was sure that someone was working against him. He was relieved to find out that there was a reason for it all."

Grandma laughed and got up to brush the crumbs from the table.

"It just shows," she said, "that you have to be careful about blaming people. You can't always believe even the things you see!"

14

The Old Door

THE SUMMER I was nine years old, Grandma and I took a trip. It was a particularly exciting trip, because we were going north to visit Grandma's old home. Of course, it wouldn't be the same log cabin that she had lived in when the Indian came to visit. Even though it was the farmhouse, and I remembered all the stories about it, everything might not look the same.

"Remember," said Grandma. "It won't be just as I've described it. Your Uncle Roy doesn't have any animals now, only the orchard. But a lot of things will be the same."

I was not disappointed. The trees along the lane were tall and made a green canopy for us to ride under. I could almost see Nellie clopping up the lane toward the barn. The old pump that Grandma had stuck her tongue on was still there, but it wasn't used anymore. There was water in the house now.

As soon as I could, I began to explore the house. In the parlor were pictures of Ma and Pa. A slippery horse-hair sofa was fun to sit on, but not very safe if I forgot to hang on. I looked through the old photograph album for pictures of Grandma when she was young.

Later, when I wandered out to the kitchen, Grandma and Aunt Julia were sitting at the kitchen table having coffee. I sat down and munched a cookie while I listened to them talk.

"I see you have a new door," said Grandma. "I guess the old one was in pretty bad shape."

"Yes," said Aunt Julia. "But Roy couldn't bear to give it up. It stands out in the barn now with dust on it. I don't know what he sees in it."

Grandma laughed. "I don't either," she said. "One of the worst hidings Roy ever got was over that door!"

I perked up to listen. Here was a story I had never heard. Neither had Aunt Julia, apparently.

"I never heard about that," she said. "What happened?"

"Well," said Grandma, "did you ever notice the bottom piece of the door had been added later? It was added after the children were all bigger. But when we were small, Pa had put a panel on the door that was on hinges. It allowed the children, the cat, and the dog to come into the kitchen without bothering Ma to run and open the door. We called it the 'cat hole.' It was really very convenient during the summer.

"The big front door was seldom ever used. A special occasion, like a wedding or a funeral, was about the only reason to go in or out the front door. People who came to visit followed the lane around to the back door and were entertained in the kitchen.

"Roy's trouble started one day when he was still quite young. The Carters had boys about the ages of Reuben and Roy, and Ma had told Mrs. Carter to send them over here to stay while she made a trip to town.

"For a while the boys were content to play in the barn and on the rope swing in the yard. Then I guess they got bored, and looked for something more exciting to do. Roy admitted that he was the one who suggested that they play a trick on Ma.

"They decided to sneak up to the front door, knock loudly, and then hide when Ma came to see who was there. The trick worked just fine. Ma was so startled to hear someone at the front door that she dropped a dish. She grabbed her fresh apron from the hook, and dashed through the house to see who it could be.

"Of course there was no one there. Ma was puzzled. She was sure the knock had been on the front door. She stood looking a moment, then returned to the kitchen. As she was cleaning up the broken dish, the knock sounded again.

" 'Maybe,' she thought, 'whoever it was thought I wasn't coming and started around the house. I'd better go see.'

"So Ma ran through the house again to open the front door. Of course, no one was there. This time, though, she caught sight of a shirt she recognized.

" 'Those boys are trying to play a joke on me,' she said to herself. 'Well, they won't catch me again.'

"Ma went back to work. The boys decided they had worn that trick out and went to the creek to play.

"Shortly before dinner time, Ma heard a knock on the front door again.

" 'Those boys,' she muttered. 'There they are again. I'll just ignore them.'

"She continued with preparation for dinner, but the knock sounded again, louder this time.

" 'Boys,' Ma called, 'I know your tricks. You go on and play. If you want to come in, come to the back door.'

"There was a pause, then the knocking began again. Ma was annoyed. They had played around long enough, she thought.

" 'Did you hear me?' she called loudly. 'You go around to the back and come in the cat hole!'

"The knocking stopped. All was quiet for a few moments. Then Ma heard a gentle voice at the back door.

" 'Sister O'Dell?' said the voice. 'I'm the new minister. Apparently I called at the wrong door. I'm a little large to come through the cat hole, but I'll try if you like.'

"Ma dropped another dish and hurried to open the door.

" 'Oh, my,' she said. 'I'm so sorry! I thought it was the boys with their tricks. My, oh, my! What a terrible thing to do!'

" 'That's all right,' laughed the minister. 'I don't mind at all. I know how boys are.'

" 'And I know how one is going to be this afternoon,' Ma thought grimly. 'He'll wish he'd never seen that front door.'

"The minister stayed to dinner, and we all enjoyed his visit. But when he and the Carter boys had left, Roy got a tanning from Ma that he didn't forget for some time!"

Grandma and Aunt Julia laughed heartily at the memory, and I ran off to find Uncle Roy. I wanted to see if he remembered that day. He did, of course, and laughed loudly.

"It's funny now," he said, rubbing the seat of his overalls, "but Ma had a lot of strength in that little arm of hers. I laughed out the other side of my mouth that day!"

In the barn, the dusty old door stood against the wall. It had seen a lot of coming and going. If only it could tell stories too!

15

Pa and the Dishwater

GRANDMA AND I were visiting her old home, and I was having fun exploring the farm I had heard about in so many stories. Uncle Roy didn't mind my tagging along with him as he went about his work, and I wanted to see everything there was to see.

As we sat at the dinner table, I listened quietly to Grandma and Uncle Roy remind each other of the good and bad times they remembered about the old house and farm.

"Well, Mabel," said Uncle Roy, "I hear you've been telling stories about me and that old door."

"Yes," said Grandma, "I thought that was too good to keep."

Uncle Roy laughed. "It was," he admitted. "And if I had time, I could tell about a time you had some trouble with Pa, too. But I have to get back to my work. I can't sit here gossiping with you ladies."

Uncle Roy left, and I turned to Grandma eagerly.

"What did you do that got you in trouble, Grandma? Do you remember?"

"Yes, I think I remember what Roy was talking about," Grandma answered. "I didn't get spanked for it, but Pa was sure disgusted."

"Tell us about it, Mabel," said Aunt Julia. "I'll just start clearing the table while you talk."

"It had to do with dishes," said Grandma. "I was still quite young as I recall. Ma didn't often leave me to do dishes alone, but occasionally she had something to do, and I managed the supper dishes by myself.

"This evening was in the winter, and it got dark early. We had no kitchen sink then, so we did the dishes on the table. When the dishes were done, the dishpan was carried out behind the chicken house and the water thrown away. Ma usually took care of this, not only because the dishpan was heavy for me, but because I was afraid of the dark. Nothing could induce me to go past the back porch by myself after dark. The boys teased me, Ma and Pa both tried to reason with me, but I was not moved. They could say what they liked. I was convinced that most anything would be lurking beyond the porch, waiting for me to come out.

"So this evening I dawdled with the dishes as long as I dared. I thought perhaps if I took long enough, Pa or the boys would come in from the barn and I could persuade one of them to take the dishwater out for me. Of course, I didn't have much faith in getting the boys' help. They would just call me 'baby' and tell Ma I was acting like a foolish girl. But Pa was usually kind-hearted; I thought I could probably get around him.

"Ma finally realized that the job was taking unusually long, and called to me.

" 'Mabel, aren't you through with those dishes yet? What's taking you so long?'

" 'Yes, Ma,' I answered. 'I'm almost through. I have to empty the water and wash the dish towels.'

" 'Well, hurry,' said Ma. 'I need to try this dress on you before I can do much more.'

"I knew my time was up. There was no sign of Pa, so I would have to brave it by myself. I opened the door, and picking up the dishpan, I held it close and backed out, pushing open that old screen door.

"Oh, it was dark out there. I shivered and thought how far it was to the chicken house and back. What if something jumped out at me? I'd probably die of fright, then they'd all be sorry.

"I stood on the porch and peered into the darkness. The longer I looked, the more sure I was that I didn't want to leave. Why couldn't I just throw the dishwater over the edge of the porch and rush back in?

"I knew why not, of course. Ma would never allow such a thing. But Ma wasn't there, and since water sank into the ground, she need never know. The idea seemed better all the time. With one look over my shoulder, to be sure she had not come to check on me, I threw that dishwater as hard as I could.

"Unfortunately for me, Pa chose that very moment to come around the side of the house. The flying dishwater hit him full in the face and ran down the front of his overalls! I was horrified. The dark didn't bother me now —I had more trouble than that to think about!

"Pa sputtered and tried to find a dry place on his sleeve to mop his face.

" 'What in the world are you doing?' he roared. 'Are you trying to drown me?'

"He stumped into the kitchen, and I followed timidly behind. Of course Ma heard the racket and came to see what had happened. Pa was wiping his hair and face with the towel and muttering something about a 'fool trick.' I was in tears, still clutching the dishpan and standing by the door.

"Ma saw at once what I had done, and she got clean water for Pa to wash his hair and face. When things had settled down a bit, Ma turned her attention to me.

" 'Now wasn't that a foolish thing to do?' she said. 'Why didn't you call me to help you, or wait until Pa came in? You ought to be ashamed of yourself!'

"I was. It wasn't much use to tell Pa I was sorry. I knew I deserved punishment, and expected to get it. However, by the time Pa was dried off, he began to see the funny side of it. I was sent to bed early, but I could hear him and Ma laughing in the kitchen. I went to sleep, determined not to do that again. The next time Pa might not see the joke, and I would be in trouble!"

Grandma and Aunt Julia finished the dishes and went to sit on the porch. I wandered out to the orchard in search of Uncle Roy, and possibly some more stories about when he and Grandma were little.

16

The Dishes

WHILE GRANDMA and I visited her old home, I discovered many things I had never seen before. One of them was a big double wooden door that sloped from the back porch down to the ground. It had two metal hinges on it, and large rusty-looking rings. I asked Uncle Roy what a door was doing there.

"That's the door to the old root cellar," he said. "We don't use it anymore, but when your Grandma and I were young, it was used to store food that needed to be kept over the winter. We can look down there if you want to."

Uncle Roy grasped one of the rings and pulled the big creaky door back. He started down the old wooden stairs and I timidly followed.

"Where are the lights?" I asked.

"No lights down here," Uncle Roy laughed. "We carried a lantern when we needed light."

The cellar was dark and earthy-smelling, and it was several moments before I could see anything. I finally made out some shelves along one wall, and a hard dirt floor. It was pleasantly cool after the warm sun outside.

"Ma kept her canned fruit and vegetables on those shelves," said Uncle Roy. "She also had baskets of apples and potatoes and onions. This was a mighty handy place."

Uncle Roy chuckled. "You might ask your Grandma what else it was handy for," he said.

I wasted no time in tracking down Grandma.

"Grandma, Uncle Roy said to ask you what the root cellar was handy for. What did he mean?"

"That Roy," Grandma said. "He doesn't forget much that I did wrong, does he? I guess he wants me to tell you about a day that I was very naughty. I don't know as I ought to tell that one."

"Oh, please, Grandma," I begged. "You couldn't have been *very* naughty. Tell me about it."

Grandma sat down on the bed with a box of things to sort, and started the story.

"It happened one day when I was about your age," she said, "old enough to know better. Right after breakfast, Ma was called to see a neighbor who was sick.

" 'Mabel,' she said, 'I'm afraid you will have to do the dishes alone. I'll have to hurry, because I want to be back before dinner time. They won't take long if you get right at them.'

" 'Oh, Ma,' I moaned. 'Sarah Jane is coming this morning, and we wanted to take our dolls down to the creek to play. Do I have to?'

" 'I'm sorry,' said Ma, 'but it can't be helped. You're a big girl, and you can help out a little. Finish your breakfast now, and get started on the dishes.'

"I slowly finished my bread and jam, thinking how unfair life was, while Ma went to get ready. I was still sitting at the table when she left in the buggy for the neighboring farm.

"Reluctantly I got up and began to clear the table. I hadn't moved very many dishes before Sarah Jane appeared at the door. She carried her doll and was ready

" 'Come on, Mabel,' she said. 'Let's hurry. We have to make our playhouse.'

" 'I can't, Sarah Jane,' I said. 'I have to do the dishes first. Ma had to go away.'

" 'Do them when we come back,' Sarah Jane suggested. 'They'll wait until then. I can only stay 'til dinner time.'

" 'Oh, I couldn't do that,' I said, 'Ma wouldn't like it. She wants her kitchen cleaned up first thing in the morning.'

"Sarah Jane came in and stood by the table.

" 'These will take you all morning,' she said. 'Couldn't you pile them in a pan and put them out of sight until we come back?'

" 'Well,' I said doubtfully, 'where would I put them? The oven is too hot, and I can't put them in the cupboard with the clean dishes.'

"We thought a moment, then Sarah Jane had an idea.

" 'How about the root cellar?' she said. 'No one would see them there. And we could get back in time for you to do them before your Ma gets home.'

"That seemed like a reasonable idea. Quickly I stacked the dishes in a big pan, wiped off the table, and started for the root cellar. It took both of us to get the big door open, but finally, after much pulling, it swung back. I ran down the steps and put the pan on the shelf. We closed the door, and I hurried to get Emily.

"Sarah Jane and I played all morning under a tree by the creek. The thought of those dishes never entered my mind again. At noon, Sarah Jane had to leave, so we picked up our things and returned to the house. Ma was back, and was busy getting dinner.

" 'Ring the dinner bell, Mabel,' she said to me. 'Pa and the boys are way at the back lot today. They'll need to get ready to eat.'

"I rang the bell, then washed and helped Ma set the table. Pa and the boys came, and we sat down to eat. About halfway through the meal, Ma went to the cupboard for a dish.

"'Now where is that little platter?' she said. 'It must have something on it in the pantry.'

"I stopped with the fork halfway to my mouth. The dishes! I had forgotten the dishes in the root cellar! What was I to do? Now that Ma was back, how could I get them washed? I suddenly had no appetite.

"'What's the matter, Mabel?' Ma said. 'Are you sick? You've hardly touched your dinner.'

"'No, I'm not sick,' I said. 'I'm not very hungry, that's all.'

"'You probably spent too much time in the sun this morning,' said Ma. 'You better stay in the shade this afternoon.'

"I intended to stay in the shade—the shade of the root cellar, as soon as I could get there without being seen. Perhaps while Ma was in another part of the house I could do those dishes.

"I hadn't counted on the fact, however, that I couldn't open the cellar door by myself. Now what could I do? No use to ask the boys or Pa to help. They would need to know why, and I would be in for it. All afternoon I moped around the porch, wishing the cellar door would open and swallow me up.

"By supper time, Ma was alarmed by my actions. When I couldn't eat, she was sure I was sick. Directly after family prayer, when Pa, as usual, prayed that the Lord would bless Mabel and help her be a good child, Ma hurried me off to bed. She was sure I was coming down with something.

"I tossed and turned in my bed. Why had I listened to Sarah Jane? What would happen when Ma found out? What made me such a wicked little girl?

"After what seemed hours to me, I could stand it no longer. I crept down to the kitchen, threw myself into Ma's lap, and sobbed loudly.

"Ma was startled. Whatever was the matter? With much sniffling, I told her the story. Those dreadful dishes were still in the root cellar, and I couldn't get them out.

"Ma took me in her lap. She was sorry to hear that I had been disobedient. However, I seemed to have suffered enough over it, so she wouldn't spank me. I did have to be punished though. I would not play with Sarah Jane any more that week.

"My heart was so much lighter that the punishment didn't seem too bad. I returned to bed with a clear conscience and a resolve to be a better girl in the future. You really do feel better when you obey your father and mother, like the Commandment says."

"And were you better, Grandma? Didn't you ever do anything naughty again?" I asked.

Grandma laughed. "I wish I could say I didn't, but that wouldn't be true. I didn't hide any more dirty dishes, though!"

17

Ma's Birthday Cake

GRANDMA WAS BAKING, and I had volunteered my services as onlooker and commentator.

"When can I bake something, Grandma?" I asked. "I'm old enough to bake by myself. I can read the recipe and measure things."

"Yes," said Grandma, "I believe you could. In fact, you would probably do a better job than I did the first time!"

Grandma laughed as she reached for the cookie pans.

"Ma was going to have a birthday," Grandma continued, "and I thought it would be a good idea to have a surprise party for her. I talked it over with Pa, and he agreed that it would be nice. We could have the party in the front yard. There were lots of trees and soft grass, and it would be an excellent place for all the neighbors to gather. How this could be accomplished without Ma suspecting, we didn't know, but we were determined to try.

"Fortune was with us, for on the morning of the party Ma discovered that she had to make a trip to town before she could finish the shirts she was sewing for the boys.

" 'Mabel,' she said, 'how would you like to go into town with me this morning? We can leave right after breakfast and be back in time to get dinner for Pa and the boys.'

"Usually I would not have been able to finish my breakfast for thinking of a trip to town, but this morning my thoughts were on the party. What luck! With Ma gone, I could make her a birthday cake!

" 'I guess I won't go this morning, Ma,' I replied. 'I think I'd rather stay here.'

"Ma looked at me with concern.

" 'Are you sick?' she asked. 'Do you have a fever?' She felt my head anxiously.

" 'Oh, no, Ma,' I said quickly. 'I feel just fine. I'll even do the dishes for you if you'd like to get started right away.'

"Ma looked puzzled, but she had no time to pursue the matter further.

"I began to clear the table and get the dishes ready to wash. This was not usually one of my favorite jobs, but today was a special day. Ma was soon ready to leave. She stopped at the door and looked at me suspiciously.

" 'Are you sure you don't want to come?' she said. 'Are you planning some kind of mischief while I'm gone?'

" 'Of course not, Ma,' I said. 'I'll be as good as can be. You don't have to worry about me.'

"Ma's look said that she *would* worry about me, but she got into the buggy, and I watched as she and Nellie disappeared down the lane. Quickly I finished the dishes and began to gather the things necessary for the cake. I knew exactly what was needed. I had watched Ma stir up a cake so many times that I hadn't the least doubt about my ability to make one too.

"The oven would present a little problem. I decided to ask Pa to fix the fire for me, and I found him in the barn.

" 'Pa,' I said, 'I'm making a birthday cake for Ma. Would you build up the fire for me?'

"Pa looked surprised.

" 'Are you sure you can do that by yourself, Mabel? You've never baked a cake before, have you?'

" 'No,' I said, 'but I've watched Ma a lot. I'm sure I can do it, Pa. Please let me try.'

"Pa was reluctant, but he came into the kitchen and fixed the fire. After giving me careful instructions about the hot oven, he returned to the barn. I began happily mixing the cake in Ma's biggest mixing bowl. I had left out nothing, I was sure. The batter looked just wonderful.

"As I greased the cake tins, I went back over the things I had put in the cake. Suddenly I remembered. The flavoring! I hadn't put any flavoring in it! Quickly I ran to the pantry and reached for the big Watkin's bottle that held the vanilla. Carefully I measured and stirred in the flavoring, and returned the bottle to the shelf.

"The cake was ready to bake. I pulled my chair up near the oven to keep an eye on things. It was a warm spring day, and I longed to be outside, but I dared not leave my cake for a moment. What if one of the boys came in, slammed the door, and made it fall? Nothing must happen to ruin this cake.

"Nothing did. It was high and golden brown. It looked every bit as good as Ma's cakes. Proudly I set the tins on the table to cool. I had only to make the frosting and hide the cake before Ma returned.

"When the buggy turned in the lane shortly before dinner time, I was swinging under the big tree. I ran to help Ma with her bundles as Roy led Nellie to the barn. I longed to tell her my secret, but of course I couldn't. This was to be a surprise party!

"If Ma suspected anything, she didn't let on. She returned to her sewing, and I spent the afternoon hanging on the front gate, waiting for the first arrivals to the party. They were to come at suppertime, and the ladies would all bring something good to eat. I was sure that no one would come with as beautiful a cake as mine, though.

"And I was right. Ma was surprised and pleased.

"'You made this all by yourself, Mabel?' she asked. 'Why, it is just lovely. I had no idea you could do that alone!'

"Proudly I handed Ma the knife.

"'You must have the first piece, because it's your birthday,' I said.

"Ma cut the cake, and took a large slice on her plate. She took a bite, and an odd look came over her face. Something was wrong, I thought. But what could it be? I watched anxiously, but Ma kept on eating. Satisfied with my success, I ran to play with the other children.

"That evening, when the last guest was gone, we sat in the kitchen talking over the surprise.

"'And the biggest surprise was Mabel's cake,' Ma said. 'It was the most unusual cake I've ever eaten. What did you use to flavor it, Mabel?' she asked.

"'Why the vanilla, Ma,' I said. 'Just like you always use.'

"'Show me where you got it,' said Ma. "Where did you find the vanilla?'

"Ma followed me to the pantry, and I pointed to the big bottle on the shelf. Ma took it down and looked at it, then she began to laugh. On the front of the bottle the label read, WATKIN'S LINIMENT.

"Ma wiped her eyes and hugged me close.

"'That's all right, Mabel,' she said. 'It was a lovely cake. A little liniment never hurt anyone. I couldn't have asked for a better birthday present.'"

Grandma put the cookies in the oven and began clearing the table. She looked thoughtfully at the Watkin's vanilla bottle.

"Those bottles do look a lot alike," she said. "I'm surprised I haven't done the same thing again. But no one except Ma would have been brave enough to eat it if I had!"

"I would, Grandma," I assured her. "I'd eat anything you made."

And I would, too. Even now, if I had the chance.

18

Grandma's Warm Clothes

IT WAS A very cold night, and the wind whistled around the windows as I started to get ready for bed.

"I hate to get in bed, Grandma," I said, "the sheets are going to be so cold."

"Bring me your nightgown," said Grandma, "and I'll iron it for you."

I brought the nightgown, and Grandma quickly ironed it. When I put it on, it felt warm and toasty, and I hurried to get in bed.

"Did your mother iron your nightgown for you when you were little, Grandma?" I asked.

"No, she didn't have to iron it," said Grandma. "We had a place on the back of the old wood stove in the kitchen where we warmed our clothes. It was always cold in winter when we got up or went to bed, because our bedrooms were not heated."

I snuggled into the covers and thought how lucky I was.

Grandma paused before turning off my light.

"That stove got a little crowded sometimes," she laughed. "The boys wanted their clothes warmed too, and poor Ma had to work around a pile of shirts and socks and scarves. In fact, I almost ruined our chances for warm clothes one time."

"You did, Grandma? Tell me what happened," I said.

Grandma sat down in the rocker.

"I woke up one morning very early," she said. "It wasn't light yet, but I could see that snow had drifted in around the window, so I knew there must be a storm, and it was going to be cold going to school.

"I heard Pa building up the fire before he left for the barn. I knew the boys would be called in a little while, and they would rush down with their clothes to warm them and dress by the fire. After they left for their chores, Ma would call me. I decided I would get a head start on them this morning, and get my clothes down to warm before they did.

"Quietly I got out of bed and gathered up the things Ma had left on the chair for me to wear that day. I tiptoed down to the kitchen, and was pleased to see that Ma wasn't there yet. I'd surprise them all. As I started to put my clothes on the back of the stove, another idea struck me. Why not put them in the oven? They'd heat faster and be much warmer to put on. So I opened the oven door and pushed in my flannel petticoats and heavy stockings. Then I ran back to my room and jumped into bed.

"A few minutes later, I heard the boys run down to the kitchen, and I listened drowsily as they talked to Ma. Before they had left the house, Pa returned from the barn.

" 'The storm is getting worse, Maryanne,' he said to Ma. 'I don't believe the children had better go to school today. Even if they took Nellie, they might not be able to get back by afternoon.'

"Ma agreed, and I heard the boys' excited voices as they left for the barn.

" 'I'll just let Mabel sleep awhile longer then,' said Ma. 'She can get up when the kitchen gets warmer.'

"This pleased me, and forgetting all about my clothes warming in the oven, I went back to sleep. It was sometime later when Ma came to call me for breakfast.

" 'Put on your wrapper now, Mabel,' she said. 'You can dress after breakfast. You won't be going to school today.'

"While we were eating, Reuben said, 'Ma, you must be standing too close to the stove. I can smell your apron burning.'

"Ma jumped back from the stove.

" 'No, it isn't burning,' she said, 'but I do smell something. Did one of you leave a mitten on the back of the stove? Maybe they fell behind.'

"Roy got down on the floor to look, but he saw nothing. By this time the odor was stronger, and Ma was looking to see if something had been put in with the wood.

"Pa got up to help search.

" 'I believe it's coming from the oven,' he said, and he opened the door. Smoke billowed out and Ma ran to open the kitchen door. Quickly Pa reached into the oven and pulled out my petticoats and stockings. The boys looked at the scorched flannel and wool, and then at Ma, who had come to survey the mess. Their smug looks said that they were glad it wasn't *their* clothes Pa had found in the oven.

" 'We'll be up to our shoetops in snow in our own kitchen,' Pa said as he went to close the door. 'Who is responsible for this foolishness?'

"Of course everyone looked at me.

" 'I just wanted to warm my clothes,' I said in a small voice. 'I guess I forgot they were in there.'

" 'You'll have more than warm clothes if you pull a trick like that again,' Ma said to me. 'Now get the broom and sweep out that snow. I declare, I don't know what possesses you to be so thoughtless.'

"Ma picked up my clothes and held them at arm's length.

" 'Hardly even fit for rags,' she said. 'My, I hope you grow up to have a little sense. It won't be safe to let you out alone if you don't.'

"I was properly ashamed and managed to be pretty quiet the rest of the day. Ma saw to warming my clothes from then on."

Grandma laughed and turned out my light. I listened sleepily to the wind and was thankful for a warm bed and a Grandma who knew such good stories.

19

Grandma's Prayer

THE DAY WAS very hot, and I flopped down on the steps where Grandma was shelling peas for supper.

"Oh, dear," I complained, "why does it have to be so hot? Couldn't we pray that the Lord would send us some cold weather?"

Grandma laughed and threw me a pod to chew on.

"It will be cooler when the sun goes down," she said. "I don't think the Lord wants us to pray for something like that. In fact, I learned that lesson the hard way."

The heat suddenly seemed a little easier to bear if there was to be a story, so I settled back on the step and waited expectantly. Grandma smiled to herself and began.

"It happened the summer I was nine years old," she said. "It was a day in August, much like this one. Pa had been up to the house several times for a cool drink, and finally said to Ma, 'I guess I'll have to give up on the fences until later. It's just too hot to work out there. But

if this heat doesn't let up so I can finish, we won't be able to get in to town on Saturday. I'll have to work early in the morning and after the sun goes down.'

"Pa returned to the barn, and I sat beside the cellar door thinking about what I had heard. Not go to town on Saturday! That just couldn't be! Sarah Jane and I had planned the whole day, and I just couldn't miss it.

"I turned the problem over in my mind for some time," Grandma continued. "What could I do about the heat? Nothing, of course. And if Pa said no trip, then it was no trip.

"After supper, Pa took down the big Bible for prayers. The Scripture he chose perked me up considerably. He read, 'If you ask anything in my name, I will do it.'

"That was the answer! I'd pray for cool weather tomorrow so that Pa could finish his fences. While Pa thanked the Lord for His goodness to us and asked His blessing on our home, I had just one request: 'Please make it cool tomorrow.'

Grandma rocked a moment as she thought.

"I awoke early the next morning," she said, "and ran to the window to look for clouds. I knew at once that my prayer was not answered. The sun was coming up, and the sky was clear. It promised to be as hot as yesterday, or perhaps even hotter.

"I ate breakfast in glum silence. Maybe I hadn't prayed hard enough. Or maybe I didn't promise enough in return. As soon as I had finished helping Ma in the kitchen, I hurried to my room to ask the Lord again for cool weather. This time I promised to be obedient, kind to my brothers, and more help to Ma.

"I was so sure I had been heard that it was no surprise to hear Ma say, shortly after noon, 'Would you look at those black clouds coming over! Mabel, run and shut the windows in the boys' room. I believe it's going to rain!'

"The sky grew blacker and a chill breeze came around the porch as I watched the results of my prayers. To tell the truth, I was becoming a bit worried. This didn't look like an ordinary rain storm to me. And it wasn't. In a few minutes, the clouds broke and it began to hail. Pep ran yipping under the porch, and I hurried inside to be nearer to Ma.

"The storm was over in a short time. Pa and the boys came in from the barn, and Pa dropped heavily into a chair.

" 'Well, Maryanne,' he said, 'that did a lot of damage to the wheat. We may be able to save some of it, but it was pretty badly beaten.'

"I didn't listen further. I ran to my room and threw myself on my bed. The wheat was ruined, and it was all my fault. What would Pa do to me when he found out? I had just prayed for cool weather, not total destruction! Probably I had promised too much this time. What would the family think of me if they knew I had brought on this terrible hail storm? I was determined that they should not find out.

"But when Pa prayed that evening, and thanked the Lord for His blessing and care, I couldn't stand it any longer. I began to sob and cry, and Ma looked around in concern. Pa picked me up and put me on his lap, and finally the story came out.

" 'Why, Mabel,' said Pa, 'don't you worry about that. Just remember that the Lord doesn't expect us to ask favors for our convenience or pleasure. A hail storm often follows a hot spell like this, and your prayers didn't bring it on.' "

Grandma picked up the pans to carry them to the kitchen.

"I was comforted by Pa's assurance," she said. "But I didn't forget that day. It taught me to pray for the Lord's will instead of demanding what I wanted."

20

Molly Blue

GRANDMA AND I sat on the front porch of her old home.
"Why doesn't Uncle Roy have animals anymore?" I
asked Grandma.

"You'll have to ask him," Grandma smiled.

Uncle Roy sat down on the steps and fanned himself
with his hat.

"Animals?" he replied to my question. "Well, I guess
the orchards take as much time as I have. And you don't
have to bring trees in every night!"

He chuckled, and his eyes twinkled as he looked at
Grandma.

"Do you remember when the cows were your job,
Mabel?"

"How could I forget?" Grandma answered. "I suppose
you still see something funny about that, don't you?"

"Well, yes," Uncle Roy admitted. "It did have its
humorous side."

He laughed, and I looked eagerly at Grandma.

"I guess I was about eight years old when Roy decided that he was too old to go for the cows," Grandma began.

" 'Pa says Mabel is big enough to bring the cows home at night,' Roy announced one evening at supper. 'And since I'm going into town with Pa tomorrow, she can start then!'

"Roy looked at me triumphantly, and I quickly appealed to Pa.

" 'I can't bring the cows in alone,' I protested. 'Molly Blue doesn't like me, and if she doesn't move, none of the others will.'

" 'You can take Pep to help you,' Pa replied calmly. 'I think you can handle it this summer. Just start early so that Reuben can milk before dark.'

"The matter was settled, and I knew better than to argue. But I was exceedingly unhappy about the arrangement. I didn't really know that Molly Blue didn't like me, but from past experience, I knew I didn't like her!

"Molly Blue was a bawler. She was forever getting her foot caught, or her head stuck in the fence, or her bell snagged on a bush. And when she did, she bawled. It was no delicate cry for help; she could be heard clear to the house. It had become my job to go to the rescue. The boys were usually in the field with Pa, and when Ma couldn't stand the racket any longer, she would call me.

" 'Mabel, go and see what is wrong with Molly Blue. That bellowing makes me nervous.'

"I would reluctantly leave my dolls and trudge to the meadow to pull Molly Blue out of whatever predicament she was in.

"As the trips seemingly became more frequent, I began to be more annoyed with Molly. When Ma called for the third time one day, I complained.

" 'There's nothing wrong with that stupid cow, Ma. She just wants company. She quits bawling as soon as I get there.'

" 'Well, go keep her company then,' Ma replied. 'I can't stand that everlasting noise!'

"So Molly Blue and I were not friends, and I did not look forward to my new job.

"True to form, Molly Blue began bawling soon after Roy and Pa had left for town the next morning. Ma looked out the door at me, and I sighed as I started across the barnyard. My feelings were not very charitable.

"Molly Blue was standing in the creek with her nose in the air, and her mouth opened wide. I noticed that she had her eyes in the direction she knew I would appear, and as soon as she spotted me, the bawling ceased. Her foot was caught between two stones.

" 'What's the matter with you, cow?' I muttered crossly. 'How come you can't do anything for yourself?'

"I waded into the stream and moved the stones. Molly Blue calmly stepped out and turned her back on me. With a look of disgust, I went back to the house.

"The rest of the day was quiet, and when Ma reminded me of the time, I decided that I would show Pa that I didn't need help with the cows after all. I left Pep dozing in the shade and started out alone.

"There were only four cows, and I knew that when Molly Blue turned toward the barn, the others would follow. I suppose I expected that she would be obliging, since I had spent so much time on her, but of course she was not. She stood placidly on the other side of the creek and stared at the scenery. I soon realized that calling would do no good; I would have to go over and prod her.

"As I waded into the water, my mind was on that stubborn cow, and not on where I was stepping. Before I knew what had happened, I was sitting in the middle of the stream with my foot turned under me. Surprised, I tried to get up and found that I could not. My foot was firmly wedged between two rocks, and try as I would, I could not move.

"I sat in the water and watched Molly chew her cud. Why couldn't she bawl now so someone would come and see what was the matter?

"The sun began to go down, and Molly Blue and I continued to regard each other darkly. I knew that someone would wonder where we were pretty soon, but my watery seat was getting more uncomfortable, and my ankle hurt terribly.

"I was right. Reuben had started to look for me.

" 'Ma,' he called, 'where is Mabel with the cows? She should have been in half an hour ago. I haven't heard Molly Blue bawling, so she can't be stuck someplace.'

" 'No,' Ma replied grimly, 'but you're going to hear someone else bawling if that child is playing down there.'

"She sailed out of the door and down the lane. Pep followed along to see the fun. I must have been some sight, my dress soaked from the waist down with creek water, and from the waist up with my tears.

"Ma always said she saw the funny side of things first, then the other side didn't hurt as much. The funny side was not apparent to me, but Ma couldn't help laughing. She hurried to move the stones, and when she saw that I couldn't walk, she quickly became sympathetic.

" 'I can't carry you, Mabel,' she said. 'You'll have to wait until I send Reuben.'

"Pep had started Molly Blue back, and Ma hurried after the cows. I waited disconsolately, wishing that I had never seen a cow.

"Reuben soon came and carried me back to the house. He couldn't resist a comment about useless girls around a place, but he and Roy both waited on me until my ankle healed."

Grandma folded the sewing she had been working on and stood up.

"Brothers are more of a blessing than not," she said. "It's too bad you don't have any."

21

Grandma and the Gun

I HAD BEEN READING one of my books to Grandma while she worked. The story was about the Pilgrims who carried guns to church to protect them from wild animals.

"Grandma," I said, "did your father have to carry a gun to church when you were little?"

"Mercy, no!" Grandma laughed. "I'm not quite that old. There were still wild animals around our place, but they didn't often come out where there were people. Pa and the boys had guns for hunting, but they didn't need them between our house and town."

"Did you ever go hunting, Grandma?" I asked.

"No," Grandma said. "I didn't go hunting with the boys. In fact, there was only one time I ever had the gun in my hands, and that was almost a disaster!"

"Tell me about it," I said eagerly.

"Well," said Grandma, "I was about nine years old. Reuben was thirteen, and he had just gotten his first gun. He was mighty proud of it, and neither Roy nor I was allowed to breathe on it, let alone touch it.

"This evening, Reuben and Pa had just come home from hunting, and we had finished supper. Pa was sitting by the door reading the Bible, and Reuben was starting his homework at the table.

"Ma said to me, 'Mabel, would you rather sweep the floor or wash the dishes tonight?'

"Of course, given a choice like that, I would rather sweep the floor. I went out to the porch to get the broom.

" 'Mabel,' Reuben called, 'close the door. It's cold in here!'

"I hadn't intended to be out there very long, but I went back and shoved the door shut. This may have been the thing that saved our family from tragedy that night, I don't know. But I do know the Lord had His hand on us all."

Grandma paused to get another pan of apples.

"I turned to get the broom, and there standing beside it was Reuben's new gun. 'Well,' I thought to myself. 'Old bossy made me shut the door, now he can't see me. He won't know that I touched his gun.'

"As quietly as I could, I picked up the gun and rubbed the smooth barrel. Since I had never held one before, I was curious to see what Pa always looked through when he held it up to his eye. I turned toward the light from the kitchen and held the gun up to my face. I don't know what happened, but somehow I pulled the trigger, and that gun jumped back and hit me in the jaw. I went sprawling on the porch, and that was the last I remembered until I awoke in the house some time later.

"Ma told me what had happened in the kitchen. The bullet came through the door and whizzed past Pa's head. Splinters from the wooden door stuck in his hair.

"Ma had just decided that the dishwater was not hot enough and had turned to carry it back to the stove. The bullet hit the table where she had been standing.

"Reuben had gotten up to get a book, and the bullet went through the back of the chair he had been sitting in.

"It all happened so fast, that for a moment everyone forgot that I was still outside. Pa rushed out to the porch and carried me in. My face was covered with blood. When they decided I hadn't been killed, but just had some teeth knocked loose, Ma's mood changed from one of fear to indignation.

" 'I declare,' she exclaimed. 'I should tan that child for a trick like that. We could all have been killed!'

" 'No, Ma,' said Reuben. 'It was my fault. I should have put the gun away. Supper was ready when we got home, and I forgot it afterward. I'm the one you should tan.'

" 'It was my fault, too,' said Pa. 'I should have taught Mabel how to handle a gun. She just doesn't know how dangerous they are.'

" 'I suppose I could strap you all,' said Ma in disgust. 'But Mabel is old enough to know better than that. If she ever gets over being so thoughtless, it will be a miracle.'

"Ma didn't spank me," Grandma concluded. "I guess she thought my black and blue face was punishment enough. But I have never had much interest in guns since then, I can tell you!"

Grandma laughed. "The Lord was good to us, to protect my family from me!"

22

What Grandma Lost

"I AM GOING TO WASH some of your sweaters," Grandma said. "If you'll get your mittens, I'll wash them, too."

"I can't find them, Grandma," I told her.

"Have you looked for them?" Grandma asked. "You wore them to school today, didn't you?"

"No, I haven't had them for a couple of days," I replied. "I don't know where I left them."

"Now that was a careless thing to do," Grandma scolded. "It seems as though you could put your mittens in your pocket where they'd be safe."

Then she laughed.

"I guess I shouldn't scold you about mittens," she said. "I lost something a lot bigger than that when I was your age."

Of course I was anxious to hear about it, so when Grandma had finished the sweaters, she sat down with her sewing and began the story.

"It was in the spring, I remember," she said. "It was an unusual day, because both Reuben and Roy were sick. Ma was quite concerned about them, and she hadn't paid much attention to me that morning. It wasn't until I was ready to go out the door that she really noticed me.

" 'Where are you going, Mabel?' she asked.

" 'Why, I'm going to school,' I replied. 'It's time to leave.'

" 'Oh, no, Mabel,' Ma said. 'You can't go by yourself You've never walked all that way without one of the boys. You'll just have to stay home today too.'

" 'Oh, Ma!' I cried. 'I don't want to stay home! I feel just fine. I can take Nellie and the buggy; then I won't be alone.'

"Ma looked doubtful, but she had the boys on her mind, so she said, 'Well, go ask Pa about it. If he says it's all right, I suppose you can.'

"I hurried out to the barn, sure that Pa would see things my way. But he was reluctant, too.

" 'I'd take you to school myself, Mabel,' he said. 'But with both boys sick, I'm behind in the chores this morning. I'm not sure you can handle Nellie.'

" 'Oh, Pa,' I said. 'You know I can. I've even driven her to town when you were along. She knows the way to school, even if I didn't show her.'

"Pa regarded me thoughtfully for a moment.

" 'I guess you can't start any younger,' he said. 'Just be careful and don't try any fancy tricks.'

" 'Oh, I won't, Pa,' I assured him. 'I'll be extra careful.'

"I ran back to the house to tell Ma that I could go, and Pa hitched Nellie to the buggy.

"I felt pretty proud, I can tell you," Grandma continued. "I didn't know of another girl at school that was allowed to bring a horse and buggy by herself. A lot of the boys did, of course. In fact, some of them just rode their horses to school.

"As Nellie clip-clopped along the road, I began to imagine what the boys would think if I should come riding up to the school house on *my* horse. They would certainly take notice of me, I was sure. The more I thought about it, the better the idea seemed to me. I began to wonder how I could manage it. It didn't occur to me at the time that I was conforming to the things that would make me popular, instead of doing what my father wanted. The temptation to be noticed by the boys was irresistible.

"I had often ridden Nellie around the farm, so that was no problem. But what could I do with the buggy?

"By the time we came to Carter's Grove, I had forgotten about Pa's warning against fancy tricks. I decided that here would be a good place to leave the buggy for the day. I would put it off the road among the trees and get it on the way home.

"It didn't take long to unhitch Nellie, but it was a little harder to push the buggy off the road. It was only a small one, but I wasn't very big. Nevertheless, I managed to push it to a spot where I thought it would be safe for the day, then I climbed on Nellie's back and continued on to school."

Grandma smiled to herself as she sewed. Then she continued.

"I was right about causing a stir at school," she said. "The girls all gathered around, and even some of the boys looked pretty envious. When we went in to school, the teacher mentioned it.

" 'Your father must trust you, Mabel, to let you come alone with the horse. You must be very careful and go straight home after school.'

" 'Yes, Ma'am,' I replied, 'I will.'

"But I was beginning to feel ashamed of myself. Pa *had* trusted me, and he certainly hadn't expected that I would leave the buggy along the side of the road. However, the pleasure of having Nellie at school kept me from worrying about it for long. I would hitch up the buggy on the way home, and no one would need to know about it.

"Sarah Jane and I rode Nellie around the school ground at noon and had a wonderful time. I even hoped that Reuben and Roy would have to stay home another day so that we could do it tomorrow.

"As soon as school was out, I started straight for home. I didn't know how long it would take me to get Nellie hitched to the buggy again, because I had never done it by myself before. Pa had expected that one of the boys at school would help me.

"I hurried as fast as I could get Nellie to move, and soon we were back in Carter's Grove. When we reached the spot where I had left the buggy, we stopped, but I didn't get down from Nellie's back. I just sat there and looked at the trees.

"The buggy was gone!

"I glanced around to see if someone was playing a joke on me, but no one was in sight.

"Nellie stood patiently waiting until I was ready to go on. There was no use standing in Carter's Grove any longer. Someone had obviously come along during the day and taken the buggy. Maybe they had even taken it home—and I was sure to have something waiting for me when I got there.

"I was a pretty unhappy little girl," Grandma said. "Besides having to face Pa, the boys would hear about it and never let me forget it.

"Fortunately, Pa was out in the field when I got home, and he didn't see me come in on Nellie. I put her in the barn, and quickly ran to the house. Ma was relieved to see me.

"'Did you get along all right, Mabel?' she asked. 'I worried about you all alone with the buggy.'

"I nodded and went into my room to change my clothes. Ma would really have worried if she had known that I didn't even have the buggy! I knew she would find out, but it seemed better to wait as long as possible to break the news.

"I was so worried about what I would tell Pa that I must have looked sick, for after awhile Ma felt my forehead.

" 'Dear me,' she said, 'I hope you aren't coming down with what the boys have. Do you feel bad?'

" 'No, Ma,' I replied, 'I feel fine. I'm a little tired, I guess.'

"I got busy setting the table for supper and helping Ma around the kitchen. Long before I was ready for it, Pa came in to wash.

" 'I see you got back safely, Mabel,' he said with his face in the washdish. 'You should have called me to unhitch for you. Where did you put the buggy anyway?'

" 'I guess I lost it, Pa,' I said in a small voice.

"Pa stopped splashing water and there was silence in the kitchen.

" 'You guess *what*?' he said in a puzzled voice.

" 'I guess I lost it,' I repeated in a smaller voice.

"Pa lifted his head slowly and turned to look at me in disbelief. The water ran off his beard, but he didn't seem to notice.

" 'Will you kindly tell me how you can lose a BUGGY?' he roared. "Nellie hasn't run fast enough to part with a buggy since she was a colt. How could you lose a *buggy*?'

"By this time I was sobbing, and Ma was taking me on her lap.

"Pa began to mop his face with the towel and stomp toward the door.

" 'I declare,' he said, 'if I had thought you could lose a buggy right out from under you, I never would have let you go this morning.'

" 'Maryanne,' he said to Ma, 'how could that child possibly lose the buggy between here and the school-house? I just can't believe it. Maybe you know something about girls that I don't know,' he ended in disgust.

" 'Let's just calm down and find out what happened,' Ma said. 'Now, tell us, Mabel, where did you put the buggy when you got to school?'

"Bit by bit I managed to sob out the story of what I had done. Pa ate his supper in silence, every so often stopping to look at me as though he couldn't believe that any daughter of his could be so foolish.

"As soon as prayers were over, Pa clamped his hat on his head, and started out to find the buggy. I waited fearfully for the sound of Nellie's hoofs on the road. So far, Pa had not mentioned what my punishment was to be, but I was sure that it would not be a light one.

"Finally, after what seemed hours to me, Pa returned with the buggy. He had found it, he said, in Carter's Grove. Some of the older boys had seen it there, and thinking I needed taking down a peg, pushed it into the woods a little farther. They were sure that I could find it, but since I hadn't gotten off Nellie, or looked beyond the spot where I had left it, I had not seen it.

"Pa sat down and looked at me soberly.

" 'Mabel,' he said, 'since you can't seem to get over the habit of being so thoughtless, we can't let you go to school alone again. If the boys have to stay home, you'll have to stay too. Maybe when you've grown up a little more, we can trust you. But for now, you'll have to be watched like a little girl.'

"Then he kissed me and sent me to bed. I felt much worse than if he had paddled me good, but it certainly made me think about my foolish tricks."

Grandma looked at me with a smile.

"Now see if you can't find those mittens at school tomorrow," she said. "And try to be more careful from now on."

23

What Did You Expect?

My GRANDMOTHER was a firm believer in prayer. She assured me that God always answered when we prayed in faith. Sometimes He said "No, not now," or, "Wait patiently," and sometimes He said "yes" immediately. I never tired of hearing Grandma's stories about her answers to prayer.

"Grandma, tell me about the time Grandpa needed shoes."

Grandma would settle back in her chair, rest her crocheting in her lap, and we would go back together to a little farm in northern Michigan.

"Well, Grandpa and I had moved to the farm. All week he worked hard to make a living for us. Your mother was just a little girl then, and your uncle just a baby. On Sundays, Grandpa preached in the little church at the Corners. None of the people who came had any more money than we did, but they were generous with chickens and fruit and vegetables. We always had lots to eat.

"But finally the day came when Grandpa said, 'Mabel, I just can't get up in the pulpit again with these shoes. My toes are coming out, and I'm afraid to move for fear someone will see them.'

"It was true. His toes were out and his mended socks could be seen taking the air. 'Well,' I said, 'we have no money for shoes and nothing to sell to get any. We'll have to ask the Lord for them.'

"Grandpa did not believe that we should ever ask the Lord for something we could provide if we set our mind to it. But shoes did seem to be out of the question, so we began praying for a pair of shoes. I am sure Grandpa thought about those shoes several times during the week, but he never mentioned them again. He went about his work on the farm, confident that the Lord would provide what was needful.

"On Saturday morning, a buggy came up our lane, and Grandpa went out to meet it. It was one of our members with a chicken for Sunday dinner. After chatting for awhile, the visitor said, 'Oh, by the way, Brother Williams, I bought a pair of shoes last week and they just don't feel right on me. I wonder if you might be able to wear them?'

"Grandpa beamed and answered, 'Yes, Sir, I certainly can!'

"The visitor was surprised. 'Why, how do you know?' he asked. 'You haven't tried them on yet!'

(I would wiggle in anticipation, for Grandpa's answer was the best part of the story.)

" 'I'm not worried about that,' replied Grandpa. 'When the Lord sends me shoes, He sends the right size!'

Grandma would chuckle and resume her crocheting.

"That's the way the Lord treats His children, you know," she would say.

While Grandma's stories thrilled me, and I had a healthy respect for her prayers, it was not until I was nine years old that I was privileged to witness an answer that convinced me that God did indeed listen when Grandma spoke.

We had been making jelly this morning, and the sun shone through the filled glasses on the table. The paraffin to pour on top was heating slowly on the stove. Suddenly, a small spark touched the paraffin, and it blazed up, igniting the wall behind the stove. Quickly the fire spread to the ceiling. Terror-stricken, I began to run toward the door. I shall never forget Grandma as she stood with the wooden spoon in her hand, and looked up at the ceiling.

"Lord, please put it out!" she said.

And He did. That very moment. Not a spark was left. Had it not been for the blackened wall and ceiling, I might have dreamed it. I stood wide-eyed and open-mouthed as Grandma began calmly to clean up the mess.

"Well, child, what did you expect?" she asked when she discovered that I still stood speechless in the doorway. "Did you think the Lord would let the house burn down around our ears?"

What had I expected? I will have to admit that had there been time to think about it, I would not have expected a miracle. Oh, yes, I knew God performed miracles. I was brought up on those stories. But for me? That was too much to presume. My first reaction had been to call a neighbor, not God.

Have you seen any miracles lately? You've never seen one? There is only one reason for that. You haven't asked! God doesn't reserve miracles for Grandmas or preachers or people who have had a lot of experience in praying. He has them ready for any of His children who call for one.

Remember though, a miracle is not something you could do for yourself. It is an "impossible" in your life. It is a spot with no out. It is for the place where your only foreseeable future is disaster. This is the time to put in an urgent request for a miracle. And this is the time, as surely as you are God's child, that you will see one.

Well, what did you expect? That's the way the Lord treats His children, you know!